David Brooks spent his earliest years in Greece and Yugoslavia, where his father was an Australian immigration officer. He studied at the Australian National University before completing postgraduate degrees at the University of Toronto. Author of five acclaimed collections of poetry, three previous collections of short fiction, four novels, and a major work of Australian literary history (*The Sons of Clovis*, UQP 2011), his first collection of stories, *The Book of Sei* (1985), was heralded as the most impressive debut in Australian short fiction since Peter Carey's, and his second novel, *The Fern Tattoo* (UQP 2007), was shortlisted for the Miles Franklin Award. Until 2013 he taught Australian Literature at the University of Sydney, where he was also the Foundation Director of the Graduate Writing Program. The 2015–16 Australia Council Fellow in Literature, he is also a renowned editor (of A.D. Hope, R.F. Brissenden) and translator, and currently co-editor of *Southerly*. A vegan and animal rights advocate, he lives in the Blue Mountains of New South Wales.

Also by David Brooks

Novels
The House of Balthus
The Fern Tattoo
The Umbrella Club
The Conversation

Short Fiction
The Book of Sei and Other Stories
Sheep and the Diva
Black Sea

Poetry
The Cold Front
Walking to Point Clear
Urban Elegies
The Balcony
Open House

Non-fiction
The Necessary Jungle: Literature and Excess
De/scription: A Balthus Notebook
*The Sons of Clovis: Ern Malley, Adoré Floupette, and a Secret
    History of Australian Poetry*

Translation
The Golden Boat: Selected Poems of Srečko Kosovel
(with Bert Pribac)

DAVID BROOKS

NAPOLEON'S ROADS

UQP

First published 2016 by University of Queensland Press
PO Box 6042, St Lucia, Queensland 4067 Australia

uqp.com.au
uqp@uqp.uq.edu.au

Cover design by Sandy Cull, gogoGinko
Cover photograph © Michael Kenna/Supervision NY
Typeset by Post Pre-press Group, Brisbane
Printed in Australia by McPherson's Printing Group, Melbourne

Cataloguing-in-Publication Data
National Library of Australia
Cataloguing-in-publication data is available at http://catalogue.nla.gov.au

ISBN 978 0 7022 5391 1 (pbk)
ISBN 978 0 7022 6633 2 (pdf)
ISBN 978 0 7022 5634 9 (epub)
ISBN 978 0 7022 5635 6 (kindle)

University of Queensland Press uses papers that are natural, renewable and
recyclable products made from wood grown in sustainable forests. The logging
and manufacturing processes conform to the environmental regulations of the
country of origin.

TABLE of CONTENTS

Paths to the City

Why do we write? What are we groping for? Are words able to penetrate the night? Are they able to go down that road we only half recall, along which we see only our own back receding in a heat-shimmer of memory? Can they truly take paths we have not ourselves taken? Bring back the lost? Such weights they carry, these things that arrive as if unbidden, or that we sometimes think we summon from nowhere, you would think they were beasts of burden, each line a caravan, setting out by moonlight over pale trackless sand, guided by half-forgotten stars. Perhaps, after all, we are something we never thought we were, affects of a language we have not the clues to decipher, its need to survive some half-forgotten track picked out in the bewildering star-encrusted firmament that shimmers and seems to cover, in inverse, the inconceivable dunes of the sky.

NAPOLEON'S ROADS

His vision, from the constantly passing bars,
Has grown so weary that it cannot hold
anything else ...
          'The Panther', R.M. Rilke, trans. Stephen Mitchell

At first I thought they were windbreaks, to shield
the vines and villages from the mistral, or else some
charming custom of the particular area in which I
found myself, a throwback to an earlier and nobler
time. More than once in my mind's eye I saw some
grand ducal or baronial carriage making graceful
progress down one of these long, tree-lined avenues
in the early autumn twilight. But no. Madame
Elizabeth told me, when I mentioned them, that
they were Napoleon's roads, the *routes Napoléon*,
and that he had had the trees planted to shade his
troops, while on manoeuvres, from the harsh high-
summer sun. The idea had stuck. Even now, she
said, almost two hundred years later, hardly a new
road was opened that did not soon have, on either
side, its long line of plane trees.

~

All through the region they run amongst vines. In winter the clipped stocks reach out for acres on either side of the avenues of trees like ranked armies being inspected by lines of silent officers, or else quietly waiting, before battle, for a signal. Watching them there is also something else that you have seen before – the regimental order, the long rows of stunted crosses, as if these too were somehow Napoleon's idea, or there had been an idea, a shape, before all of it, running through Napoleon's veins.

~

At the Jardin des Plantes there is no panther, only a couple of aged lions in an ancient cage at an inter-section of paths with a commanding view of the broad, central avenue. They do not pace, as the panther might, but sit at the base of their large rocks, looking out over the sparse winter crowds, with rheumy eyes that, it suddenly occurs to me, might well be half blind.

Another day, walking back towards the fifth *arrondissement* from the Gare d'Austerlitz, we pass the Jardin on the river side and find we can see clearly into the cage of wolves from the Cévennes. It is 4 p.m. The traffic is heavy on the Quai Saint-Bernard. The wolves are relentlessly pacing out a large figure eight, over their small hill, down the other side, along the bottom end of the enclosure, back up the hill to cross the path they have just taken, then down on our side, along the fence, back up, crossing the path, down. Watching them, I am glad there is no panther, that he is out there somewhere, long dead, free of the cage. Paris is freezing. As we set off towards the hotel the wind picks up and an icy rain starts. I imagine the wolves pacing just to keep warm.

~

Napoleon's roads are very straight and very dangerous. There is little room to manoeuvre. Drivers in this country have a lust for speed and for passing the car in front of them – a kind of wild impatience behind the steering wheel that is probably the inverse of their famous grace and civility in the office and drawing room. They are *sauvage*, my landlady says, and will tailgate recklessly, overtake in almost impossible places. With large trees every five metres or so, on either side of the road and only centimetres from the bitumen, there is no margin for error. Where in another country a slewing or swerving car might veer into an open field or ride up onto pavement, here there is only almost certain death, wrapped around one of Napoleon's trees.

~

Coming home from Montpellier long after sunset, nearing the turn-off, using low-beam behind a car some four hundred metres in front of us, its light caged in by the long, straight avenue of trunks and winter branches, it is as if we are speeding through a tunnel far underground, or perhaps a vein, an artery in the night. 'Do we have to take the turn-off,' my daughter asks me, 'can't we keep going? I love driving at night.' As if, after all that, there would still be home at the end of it. Or this were home for the moment, this warm capsule, flying through the dark body of things.

~

A web – *une toile d'araignée* – with Paris at the centre. *Abandonnée?* Or does the web still invoke the spider?

~

The first of the roads between the D32 and Puilacher, the one closest to Canet, is only one car wide but still has its row of plane trees along either side. To let past a car that is coming the other way you have to pull over to the very edge, almost into the ditch between the road and trees, or back-up a hundred metres to the highway, running an even greater risk of ditching yourself. We call this road the stink road because of the large dam beside it, full of foul-smelling tailings from the winery. On warm days when the smell is worst we try to avoid the road entirely, or else quickly wind up the windows, drive along it holding our breath.

~

They are pulling up the road to Claremont in preparation for the new autoroute. Now, instead of the great trees between Canet and the Nébian turn-off, there are only the trunks, cut into segments, and the enormous, ploughed root-balls, almost lost, at sunset, in the gathering shadow below the pylons.

~

On the vast plain between Paris and the sea, the roads to Chartres are lined with tall poplars, bare winter branches interlacing high over the bitumen, the cathedral at the hub, stone branches at its nave and narthex just touching, as if the builders had been dreaming of poplars, or the tree-planters dreaming of the high gothic arches, the tracing in the rose windows that seems to remember the way the winter branches, interlocking over the roadway, are like a three-dimensional map of roads in the sky, seen from far off.

~

Late autumn, the harvest long over, the trimming and uprooting of stocks well underway, the cuttings and dead leaves raked into the ditches or piled in open spaces and set alight. But some of it is out of hand. Tonight eleven large blazes visible from the Paulhan turn-off alone, the fire brigades from Clermont, Gignac, Paulhan, Le Pouget all out. Sirens everywhere. And the police, driving slowly along the darkening vine-roads, looking for a culprit.

~

In London, up from the Languedoc and eating
Lebanese at the Gallipoli Café, I try to tell my
English friend about Australia. We are talking
about Shakespeare and she doesn't quite see. She
tells me about the great oaks and beeches and
plane trees. I try to tell her how they line the
roads, how dangerous and complicated this is,
how they section and shut out the countryside
about them, but she can only see the trees, how
ancient and solid and majestic they are, how nobly
they mark out the land. Later, driving back to our
borrowed flat – past Piccadilly, Trafalgar Square,
the Smithfield Markets, all those old names – I
remember what I had wanted to say as she spoke
to me: how the great oaks and beeches of the
New Forest were cut down to build the ships
that discovered Tahiti and New South Wales,
how on the Federal Highway, between Goulburn
and Collector, there runs an avenue of poplars
('*piboule*', Madame said – we are living on the
Avenue de la Piboule – 'that is old *languedocien*
for poplar') remembering the soldiers killed in
Amiens, Arras, Gallipoli. And how, beside them,
someone has started to grow vines.

~

My daughter has an image that amuses her, of the
Emperor on his days off, with a shovel and a cart
full of saplings, trudging along the roads between

the grapevines, doing the planting himself. Did Napoleon get the armies to do it, we wonder, or was it gangs of prisoners, or perhaps of labourers forced away from their vineyards for the job? And if prisoners, what kind would they be? Common criminals? Political prisoners? Prisoners of war? It's like the Great Wall of China, I tell her, and perhaps not; the different work sites, different regional commands, the construction piecemeal, the intention to connect it all at last some time far into the future ('You start from Béziers, on the way to Pézenas; others will be starting at Montagnac, Saint-Jean-de-Védas, Gignac ...

Car headlights, far back, in the rear-view mirror, like a large cat's eyes in the darkness, and I think, that's how they are, or we, coming and going, from Paulhan to Bélarga, Canet to Plaissan, if seen from out there: the panther, pacing back and forth, behind the bars of the trees.

Approaching the Intermarché just north of Canet, along the short stretch of older trees before the river, we are passed by a speeding ambulance and twenty minutes later, coming home, find it again, with two others and a police van in a cluster blocking half of the highway. One car, front badly crushed, is still on the road and the other that had been trying to pass it is badly crumpled on its side in the ditch. There are enough people there already. I am concerned only to drive slowly past and cannot look, but my daughter tells me they are taking a bald man out of the car in the ditch, that they've had to cut the car open to do so. The accident is just around the corner from the stink road and we take it into Puilacher, winding up the windows against the smell.

~

On a hill beside Plaissan is a dolmen, though you do not get to it from Plaissan but from Le Pouget, up a long dirt track and then through thickets of some wiry brush I don't manage to get a name for. A depression, or trench, or wide grave, the earth held back by giant stones to create a narrow space for the body, though whose body no-one can say: a chieftain perhaps, two thousand years ago. And around it – you can take in almost a full circle if you stand on the huge lintel – the roads, with their snaking, parallel lines of trees, in some pattern you would need a balloon to see properly. And perhaps, if you could, other hills, other dolmens. Nazca. A summoning. Except that the tombs remain empty, pieces of text, waiting.

~

Dogs on the road. Running towards me with no intention of stopping. A game of chicken. So that

I have to slow down, pull over to let them pass
in their rush to get wherever they are going. Part
of a hunting pack, lost, or on the scent of something, the rest of them somewhere out amongst
the vines. Up in the hills they are hunting deer
and wild boar, but here it is rabbits, quails bred
for the purpose, released into the vines after the
vendange, two weeks before the season starts.
When you go out walking, they say, wear bright
colours, stick to the paths.

~

The problem with a question is that it implies its
own answer. The problem with an answer is that
it responds to a question. But the question that
rejects its own answer? The answer that will not fit
its question? The memory of the tidal flats about
Mont Saint-Michel, and in the fields beyond them
the stands of trees, ranked, silver in the winter
light, like fragments of roads long washed away, or
that never came, answers to a question no-one ever
got around to asking.

How do you write like sand?
How do you write like water?

~

… Artarmon, Clovelly, Clontarf, Vaucluse …')

~

11

To see the other roads, the other trees, is not easy. You must risk your life. Particularly if you wish to take photographs. You must pull to the side, half on and half off the bitumen, on the thin strip of unmown grass that sometimes runs between the ditch and the road itself, or turn on to one of the service paths of the vineyards. Or else come to a dangerous halt in the middle of the road itself, hoping that you can finish and be driving again before the next car comes. Bearing in mind that when you're moving you can think yourself the only driver on an otherwise deserted road, and when you stop you're likely to find that within a minute or not very much longer a second car will pass and then a third. Bearing in mind, too, that unless you stop, unless you risk your life, you may never see, in that articulated sky-map of winter branches, a large crow landing, shaking the whole, or a flight of swallows darting through, straight from a meal among the vines.

~

I am beginning to drive like a Frenchman, my daughter tells me, taking greater risks, judging distances more finely, passing when there's no need to, driving at 120 in the 100 zones. I want to tell her about Rimbaud, his *dérèglement de tous les sens*, *'long, immense et raisonné'*. But it is not that. I have no excuse. The way, waking late at night, I can sometimes hear my blood, raging down its avenues. The way, not waking, I sometimes dream a dream of earliest childhood, in the Humber with my mother and father, somewhere between Belgrade and Zagreb, the rain, the long straight road, the long avenues of trees. The heart like a creature pacing inside the cage of bones. Things I cannot say, cannot retrieve.

~

Outside Canet, where the road narrows before the bridge, the great bruised trees, or by the Gignac crossroad in ghostly light, like scared men running, or the already-crucified, mile after mile. Spartacus. No unknown but we try to cage it, as if that were our greatest fear, the loose.

Driving into town on a Tuesday evening, on the road towards Gignac, I become aware of a giant moon and have to struggle to keep my eyes off it, to keep the car on the road. I have never felt the moon's power so strongly, so dangerously. All the way to the autoroute it comes and goes, strobing through the avenue of trees, slipping now behind a hill and appearing again, suddenly, through a cloud of vine-smoke. In Montpellier, at the café below the Aqueduct, safe amongst the buildings, I feel lucky to have survived – as if, very physically, something that had been pulling at me had at last let go.

~

How to say that these roads are about what is not road, this text about what it is not? In the apartment on the Avenue de la Piboule there is an aerial photograph of the surrounding countryside and the villages of *Les Six Clochers* – Puilacher, Tressan, Bélarga, Canet, Plaissan, Le Pouget – in such detail that we can see the roof of our own building; the tree-lined roads like dark ribbons through the lighter quadrilaterals of the vineyards, the unlined roads and paths amongst them a lighter and finer filigree. The *routes Napoléon*, then, and the openness beyond, the paragraphs of vines, whiteness.

~

The road outside Capestang, or over the river at Trèbes above the ranked barges. There is a sudden turn there, as the highway that has been straight for five or six kilometres, suddenly narrows, enters the village, and you cross the bridge – and calm, a moment's slowness after the speed, the majestic trees bending over the water, forming a great bower, the thin, winding streets, the café, the *tabac*, the *boulangerie*, before highway again, out through the acres of vines.

~

The plane and the poplar are fast-growing trees, but even Napoleon, planting them along his roads, can't have thought they would be tall enough to shade his troops the next year, or for several years to come. What was it then? Investment? Empire?

Belief in the future? Each year, when they did go on manoeuvres – those who lived, those who survived – the trees were a little taller, a little fuller of foliage. I imagine them singing as they marched, though perhaps it was harsher than that, only the occasional soldier, singing under his breath.

~

Thursday, 5.15 p.m., huge moon above Campagnan, round and full and riding low over the scattered lights. Impossible to return the next night but there at the same time Saturday, with camera. No moon. Have clearly miscalculated the rising times. Decide to pull off the road and wait anyway, to see. And within two minutes a police car appears – I can just make out the '*Gendarmerie*' sign in the half-dark – and moves carefully up beside me. One of them – there are three men in the car – winds the window slowly down as I do the same. Does he think I have a shotgun? Matches?

'*Un problème?*'

'*Non, pas de problème … J'attend un photo*', holding up the camera, '*– de la lune …*'

'*D'accord*', he says, calmly – not the slightest reaction – and they drive off.

God knows what they say. Maybe nothing. The moon, after all, is a remarkable thing. Even *gendarmes* watch it. Or might have – I think as I drive away – an hour ago, as they paced the D32, huge and dangerous through the bars of the trees.

THE CELLAR

He sometimes thought it was to avoid her but it wasn't. If it was to avoid anything then it was to avoid everything, but he wouldn't have said that.

The cellar had always been there, the idea of it. An openness under the house. A cool, dark space, with the damp earthen smell of a cave. Some sort of presence, or unconsciousness, and if you listened closely enough – as he had discovered the first time, clambering in through the hole under the veranda – the faint sound of trickling water. It had been precarious, that first time, climbing down, not knowing where to put his feet, only the thin blade of torchlight bouncing about: down the face of a granite boulder into the sea of broken bricks and rubble that turned out, as best he could understand it, to be the remains of the house that had been there before, collapsed into its foundations to save the cost of carting it away, so that there was no knowing, until you removed it, how deep was the hole really.

It was this that had intrigued him and played on his mind, a sort of deferred planless plan to one day find out how deep it was and make a cellar, to store wine or use as a darkroom, or just as a place to put away the kinds of things that one puts away in the dark underneath, old bassinettes and wooden-barred cots and tricycles and trainer-bikes and steamer trunks full of old uniforms, not that, as it had turned out, there had been children, or uniforms.

So that when in '96 they were having a new set of shelves built in the kitchen he'd had the carpenter cut a hole in the floor of the boot-closet under the stairs and put in a trapdoor and a wooden ladder though he, the carpenter, had been uneasy about the unstable rubble at the base and had dragged in an old piece of eight-by-four to firm it. Then in '04, with a light now installed, he – the subject of this story, not the carpenter – had rented at first a small mini-skip and then a larger one and then a larger still and had spent half a year of Sundays getting rid of the rubble, the floor getting gradually lower and lower and the unstable base of the ladder more and more of a problem until he replaced it with a longer one so he could adjust the angle as the floor descended until at last, just as he'd hoped, he found solid rock. In some places it made him think of the back of a large cetacean part-surfaced from earth-ocean, around the edge of which, from the front of the house running directly down and back into the last remaining pool of rubble, there now ran and had probably always run a trickle that in periods of heavy rain he could almost call a stream. It gave him a delicious feeling, getting up in the middle of the night and staring out at the upper branches of the huge Sydney Blue Gum, *Eucalyptus saligna*, in the moonlight from the third floor window, thinking that far beneath – a dozen feet below street-level – a small spring trickled, bathing and feeding the roots.

But how to preserve it, the stream, while at the same time turning the sub-floor space into a cellar truly? Reluctantly (but it was not without precedent; it had happened with the Tank Stream), he decided to bury it alive, and channelled the water into a PVC pipe. There was still, where the ground seemed to fall suddenly away, a part of the sub-floor covered with rubble.

The stream disappeared into it as into a pool. He realised that if he poured sand over it the sand might clog the water's exit point, wherever that was. If he was to concrete the floor it might, in this part, be as simple a matter as a plastic sheet and some sand levelled over it. It took some time – he did it in stages – but within two months he had laid a concrete floor, created a large cellar almost half the floor-size of the level above it, and was now thinking of fixtures. Perhaps a wall, dividing the space into two, with a door, on one side the wine cellar and on the other, furthest from the ladder, the darkroom, with a light outside to indicate when he shouldn't be disturbed. Not that he really expected his wife would ever come down. Once set up with a bench and chair, an enlarger, developing trays; once water had been connected (but how to drain it?), he could disappear into it for hours.

The water was a problem. Not the drainage from the sink, but the stream, or what had been the stream. Mounting behind his back during the winter. Since other things had distracted him, and the work had been suspended. A period of months when he did not go down. There was, after all, nothing stored there yet, nothing as yet that he needed to go down there to fetch.

It was a dream that alerted him. Hard to explain, or would have been, had there been anyone he needed to explain it to. A murmuring, like an actual human voice trapped. He was out of the city when he heard it, in a motel in a dry country town, at three or four in the morning, on the edge of the desert. As he drove to the next town the following day, three hundred kilometres of almost-straight road, he thought of it continually. It seemed like a sign but there was no telling of what.

Back in the city, however, it was days before he remembered and went down. And there it was, covering the concrete slab. Four or five inches of it. A dark pool which, when the trapdoor was opened, before the light was turned on, turned suddenly into a mirror in which he could see himself, in silhouette, with the light from upstairs behind him. He had no idea where it had come from. Perhaps, all along, the walls had been seeping when it rained heavily, but in the past, before the concrete, it had gathered to form the stream and so no-one had ever noticed. But now something had to be done. Maybe the stream had murmured for a reason. He brought down a crowbar, went to the part of the floor above the rubble-pool, and broke a hole in the concrete. When he went down again the next day the water had gone. He could now put in a drain, perhaps, so that the problem would not recur, but when he shone a torch into the hole, down past the concrete and the drooping, sand-covered plastic, he found that the rubble had receded. Perhaps the stream had done it. There was a gap, now, as deep as his forearm. A lair. He half-expected to find some creature in it.

The concrete was thick but would not hold indefinitely. If he filled the space with sand or rubble there was no guarantee that it wouldn't recede again and that that part of the floor wouldn't collapse. He broke more of the concrete away and began to remove the rubble. When the pile beside the hole grew large enough and as yet there was no sign that the rubble was coming to an end, he hired another skip. It seemed clear now that all along the water had been disappearing into a fissure in a large sandstone boulder – another drifter in the sea of the earth that was now all around him. But no, it was going around and under it, disappearing further down. It was almost summer again. Upstairs, when he looked out at the smooth, flesh-pale branches of the great Sydney Blue Gum late at night, he fancied he could see in one of its highest forks the shape of a possum staring out over the wide basin of the suburb in the moonlight.

From time to time as he worked he could hear his wife upstairs, moving about.

It was a room, or could have been. The size almost of the small laundry two floors above. And he found that the idea of it would not leave him alone. Having cleared it out, having found its dimensions, it seemed a question, almost a demand that had to be answered. He went down and sat there, on a three-legged stool he had brought from the garage. In the depths of the earth, had he been able to slow down his hearing – to slow it down, or perhaps it was to speed it up; he couldn't tell; from a second, say, to a thousand years – it seemed to him that he would be hearing the songs of the great boulders as they swam so darkly and slowly. A deep, deep moaning. The rumble of an elephant, he had read, although inaudible to human ears, could be heard far, far off by other elephants. Whales made sounds that travelled hundreds of kilometres through the ocean.

There seemed no choice but to make it larger, as if, having imagined it, there was nothing he could do but bring it about. The work was hard, dragging buckets of earth and stone up to the cellar level, to then fill the bins that could be dragged up and out to the skip. Sorting them first, conserving the full and the half-bricks, since if he were to make a wall it seemed logical to make it with what was already there. It took weeks, interrupted as it was by trips away. Now and then he would make, to her, some comment by way of explanation. Usually to do with finding the track of the water. He was surprised that she didn't ask questions. Before long the cavity was almost the size of the master bedroom. But further back; only part of it actually below the cellar; another part – at least half, by his calculation – under the western foundation, maybe five metres below the fence, in the direction of the Sydney Blue Gum.

He had started to think, rather dispiritedly, about another concrete floor, trying to work out how he might avoid a repetition of the water problem, when he noticed that a neighbour two doors down on the other side of the street was having his veranda-boards replaced. The ends of most of the old ones had rotted, but these could be easily sawn off. Good, sound Tallowwood, *Eucalyptus microcorys*. With a careful placement of beams beneath them they could be the makings of a wooden floor. He moved them in, beams and veranda-boards both, on a Sunday while she was out at the end-of-financial-year sales. By the time she returned there was hardly a thing left to be done, and little trace at all that anything had been. A floor. Hasty, yes, but a floor nonetheless. A plateau. An even surface to think upon. To sit on, on the three-legged stool, and plan walls, a trap-door above, some more permanent access than the old wooden ladder he had used so far.

Work distracted him again. Travelling. Motels in country towns. Tightness. Squareness on the ground. The gravelly solidity of the earth beneath. Now and then he would be given a room on a first floor, but that was only a sleight of hand, barely relief at all. In truth there was no escape. Not that way. Nor in the car, out on the plains. Everything horizontal. Everything visual. Even the sky seemed stubborn. Now and then he would stop, when he found one, at a grove of tall trees, turn off the car, walk out, stand still, try to hear water. Through the flies and the noise that most people seemed to mistake for silence.

It was a month before he could go back down to sit in the semi-darkness and listen. Here and there roots hung out from the walls. At first he had thought to cut them but then, feeling their toughness and their moisture in his hands, thinking of the huge Sydney Blue Gum that had probably been there since before the house had been thought of, had decided to leave them be. The walls that he would build from the bricks he had emptied from the space could be made around them, with gaps and crevices wherever the roots seemed to need them. It was slow work. Months went by. He installed the second trapdoor, rigged it so that a light would go on when it was lifted, fixed an iron bar to the frame onto which to hook the new, aluminium ladder so that it could be left permanently in place.

She didn't seem much interested. He said that he was building walls. There was no secret anymore. She hated ladders. If he was happy enough with whatever he was doing then she was happy enough to leave him to it. Besides, her knee was bad; she might fall if she tried to go down. And how, then, would he get her out, with the bulk of her?

One night he woke and realised that rain had come. He lay there listening to it, heavy and long, the muffled roar on the iron roof, the torrent in the gutters and downpipes. An hour, two, and the first runnels would be reaching the sub-floor, the stream would be waking. He tried to envision it, thinking the whole system through, saw water seeping up through the floorboards, inching up the feet of the ladder, felt an anxiety mounting. It made no difference to know that at this hour there was nothing he could do, or that left just a day or two any problem would most likely sort itself out. It was the knowing of it, how it came. He got up, felt his way out of the bedroom, listening before he closed the door, to see if the pattern of her breathing had changed, but could hear nothing but rain.

The cellar was dry. The walls also. When he lifted the second trapdoor, fully expecting a flood below, he found that the floorboards, too, were dry. He climbed down, sat for a while on the stool, wondering whether he could hear the rain down here. Nothing. He thought, illogically, that he might hear better, be better able to concentrate, in the dark. He climbed up, closed the trapdoor, felt his way back to the stool. As he sat there he became conscious of a tiny chink of light coming up from between the floorboards, like the light of a farmhouse seen at night from the air, ten thousand feet up, or the light from the end of a tunnel.

This third room was harder and, since he had no reason for it other than this self evident but inexplicable call, more secretive, not that there was anyone to keep the secret from. There was soil now, no rubble, and barrier stone – earth dolphins – and with the skip gone he had to dispose of it by other means. He would bring it up, in buckets, to the cellar proper, then when she was out, distribute it around the garden. The scallops of stone – for it did come away, under the chisel, in curved, creamy scallops – he piled along the side of the room above, the second one, where as yet he had still to complete the wall. This third room would not need to be large, nor was there any rush to finish. He dug down at first, and then, when there was room to stand, outward, towards where, above, he imagined the fence would be. The space was two metres deep and almost a metre-and-a-half square when he made his discovery and began slowly – it was more, now, a matter of washing than of digging – to remove the soil from around it, to reveal its smooth, white nakedness. Just as far as the needs of the room went, the aesthetics, not wanting to damage or, any more than he might already have done so, interfere.

It went on. As she explained to the police, and as she would repeatedly to others in the years that followed, she had grown used to his absences, sometimes for whole days, from the mornings until late at night, but after two days on the occasion in question had realised that something must have happened, that he must have had a heart attack, or stroke, and, if he wasn't dead already, must be lying there, unable to cry out. In truth it did not greatly trouble her. She felt she hardly knew him these days. But she knew that she would be held accountable. She could see that he wasn't at the foot of the ladder, and when she stood at the top of it and called his name there was no response.

The police, when they came – a man and a woman, both very young – went down and explored for a few minutes, then returned, unhooked the ladder, and took it away to some other part of the cellar. At first she heard some noises and muffled conversation, then silence. When they came back they said they could find nothing. There was a second room, they said, like a cellar beneath the cellar, that had a trapdoor that tripped a light when it was opened, but there was no way down. That was why they had needed to move the ladder. When they got down there they found another trapdoor, a third one, in the corner, and another room below that, but when they moved the ladder again and went down into this third space they found only a stool, and a ladder set up against one of the walls, on the other side, away from the trapdoor, where the big root was.

'It's very peaceful down there,' the young policewoman said, and paused for a while, before advising her to contact Missing Persons, which she did, and filled in all the forms. Her husband was obviously somewhere else. They needed a photograph but although he must have taken thousands she could find very few of them, and almost nothing of him. The one she gave them was at least fifteen years old. It was from one of his trips out west. He was standing under a huge gum tree (it was a *Eucalyptus camaldulensis*), on top of a hill, with a wide valley behind him. She didn't know who had taken it. Nor, she thought, was it very much like him, not really.

'KABUL'

From one of the narrow side streets, an old woman
ambles into the parking lot, squats and defecates
between the cars. It is midday, Aix, the city of
dogs. We are only feet from the main thorough-
fare, only a block from the Hôtel Casino. No-one
else sees. As she passes, her dress still caught up

25

behind her, she glances at me as she might at a bird or parked car – or rather her eye falls upon me, without interest or defiance.

'Sophia,' the night porter says – I have not told him what I have seen, merely asked about the old woman in the square: 'That is Sophia,' as if she were well known in the town, as if he were pleased I had noticed her.

~

The nurses, if that is what they are: I cannot tell how many, or what is going on behind them, further into the shadow beyond the wide, open doorway of a barn or ancient stone warehouse. They are standing around a large bench that may be an operating table, perhaps a mortuary slab. One holds up her gloved hands as if in defence or surrender, or simply to keep the blood from falling on the stone. Another's hands hang by her side. Between them, on the table, head falling back from it as if to look blindly towards me – as if he or she is too long, too tall for the space they're laid upon – is a man or a woman, I cannot tell which, only see, too far away to identify, a ghost-pale face, upside-down, and long black hair hanging limply from it, stark against the white of the sheet. Some of the nurses (*are* they nurses?) look up in my direction, as if sensing that somewhere out there in the desert heat – perhaps in the old bus that is slowly negotiating its way through the crowded square – someone is watching them.

They are all wearing the same long gloves, bloodied almost to the elbow. Just as they slip from my view – just as the bus turns left at the corner of the square – one of them seems to reach deep into the body cavity. Correspondence. The beginning of a trail. A turn-off, between paragraphs, into the whiteness beyond.

I cannot tell why I think this is Kabul. The dust, perhaps, or light. When I think of Kabul there is not, at first, a great deal to remember. Some talk I once heard of a restaurant there, where travellers on the Asian Highway gathered; an image I once saw of a merchant standing on a cobbled street; stalls of carpets and brass-ware stretching out behind him, towards the vanishing-point.

The older Kabul, before the disaster, before the invasions.

~

My friend tells me there is cannibalism in Kabul. The tense puzzles me. I would understand it better if he said *there had been*, as perhaps there was in the time of the civil war, the siege by the Russians, the Mujahideen. But *there is* is a different matter. So much so that I think he is saying something else, something quite other than that.

~

Dry. So dry. When a shell hits there is mainly dust, small puff-clouds seen through binoculars. No particular target, unless rocks, hillside, something buried or dug in there, silence. And roads to the city, four of them, snaking out over the vast plain. Lorries, jeeps, trucks, sometimes carrying small platoons, sometimes farm produce, sometimes prisoners, often only the dust.

~

> She told me that it was alright if I wanted
> to hurt her, but I didn't. There was blood
> everywhere – over the sheets, the pillows, my
> hand – but it wasn't that. She had to leave the
> next day, she said, and by noon she was gone.
> I wrote but there was no answer. The next
> time I was in the city I left a message, but
> she didn't return my call. When I found her
> apartment I thought I heard a sound inside,
> but when I knocked the door stayed closed.
> I was confused: if I had hurt her, would she
> have stayed?

~

At a dinner party I meet someone who has lived in Kabul. I ask him about the cannibalism but he is sceptical. He reminds me of the Zoroastrians, the Parsis and the Temples of the Dead, the wooden platforms, exposure of bodies to the birds. Vultures eat the flesh of humans, he says, most certainly, but humans do not. An operation, on the other hand, or post-mortem, these things were possible, given the exigencies of wartime. If, that is, it was not merely a dream; if I saw what I saw at all.

~

> P. is a dark place, or was that winter, and cold, right through to the bones. An upper and a lower city, set on and around the hill. Arches, colonnades, places where people can meet in secret. A broad, cobbled avenue leading to the main piazza. Rude waiters, avaricious landlords. And at the end of a dark side street the long staircase down to the Street of the Minotaur and its musty hotels, sad attic spaces, proprietors reluctant to show you their rooms because they know that you will not stay. A long, long staircase, almost a thousand steps.

~

*Ka*bul? Ka*bul*? I have heard it both ways, as if there were two places, split by the tongue. Is it necessary to know the actual city? Or would knowledge of the actual city mask the other, prevent us again from arriving? Entry from Pakistan or Iran is not easy. There are border-posts. And within the borders, sieges, checkpoints, further borders. When the city is occupied by one force, it is the other force that prevents us. *If the city could be entered it would not be the city.* Hence the dependence upon fragments, fortuitous glimpses: any other kind would undo itself. *Why would I go there*, my friend writes, *if I could imagine it?*

~

We see it repeatedly over the years, whenever something within us draws our attention there, as if it were a need, a part of us – images of people in makeshift hospital beds, their bloodied stumps balled in thick bandages, children growing up without hands, feet. There is violence even in the metaphor, if that's what this is, but perhaps that is the point; people straining out of the skins of themselves; in every construction, every artefact, these moments of rupture.

~

In a book about Charles Sobhraj, the gem-dealer-drug-runner who murdered so many on the Asian Highway, I read about how he and Chantal were imprisoned in Kabul – how he escaped, in pyjamas, onto the Street of the Carpetsellers, and went to Paris, leaving her in prison. How he drugged her mother at the Paris Hilton to get his own daughter back, then was caught again and spent a year in a Greek prison before returning to Kabul, only to find Chantal gone.

~

A sparrow has flown in through one of the large open windows and is hopping about between the restaurant tables under the feet of the waitresses. Out on the square a couple in their mid-thirties are arguing. They are trying to keep their voices down but their anger is evident. First one moves a pace or two away and the other follows, and then it is the other who moves away, as if the anger itself were a rope, only three or four metres long, tying them together, or this were a dance of prisoners.

~

Late at night, unable to sleep, I find myself thinking about Sophia: how, when I was leaving the city, I saw her sleeping on her pile of rags in the white marble entrance to the Crédit Agricole. How I found her again, in a dream, on the long flight of stairs: the rushing, the pool of light, the people grouped about her body. How the stairs continued downwards, into a further dark that the dream did not let me bring anything back from. How I had realised, years later, that this dream may have meant that she was dying, that all along I might have known this without knowing. How there is no-one, after all, no-one to tell.

~

A television has been left on in an empty room. On the screen, several men are standing by a well in which they have just discovered the victims of a massacre. Some of the men have cloths over their mouths and noses, to shield them from the smell. I almost said 'over their faces', as if to shield them also from the sight, as if to shield them from knowing.

~

It is not always the body, not only. Kabul is within us, but is also a landscape of the days, a positive to their negative, a trace. Weeks marked by craters, explosions of shells. Months marked by lies and betrayal. A field map of engagements, tracks leading inland. (There, on those ridges, a hide-out. And, if you could get to it, a view of the city. The minarets, the domes, convoys moving in or out. The land dry. The puffs of smoke where the shells hit. Or in winter, when it is covered with snow ...)

~

On one side of the great plug of stone upon which P. sits – you could not call it a hill – is a rent or fissure like a crack in a curtain, though the men in the city have always had another name for it. Seen from the outside it looks to be the opening of a large cave, the entrance to an underworld, but in fact it is far taller than it is deep, and the people of P. several centuries ago tunnelled down from the main piazza to create a set of long staircases, hidden from their enemies, by which they could enter or leave the city. The modern city has widened the tunnel and replaced most of the stairs with escalators. You can see, each morning and evening, a long procession of people of all descriptions, standing almost stock still as they are taken up or down into the darkness.

~

We exchange what we know: the long civil war, the damage, the landmines that turned the Dasht-i-Margo into the Desert of Death. I talk about the Taliban and the restoration of the holy law, the executions, the severing of hands, the ineptitude of the peasant government. He tells me how the population undermines it – the small flashes of colour, the eyes – but is also grateful for the peace, a kind of hard certainty after the terror. Again Kabul is not the subject, or is, unexpectedly. One of us is weeping. *There is nothing to do but damage*, I tell him, but even as I say it I know it is the damage speaking.

~

We are in Kabul now, at the Intercontinental. The weather is hot and the airconditioning is not working. The electricity goes off at night and for some stretches during the day. There is talk of rebels in the hills but the hippies seem

*to get through. You can buy lumps of hash in
the markets for a song, good, rich stuff, and
all sorts of drugs at the pharmacies. But the
problem is getting it out, and there's a limit as
to how much you can use while you're here. I
prefer the icy vodka martinis, and the bar is a
better way to meet people ...*

~

Cannibalism, they say, is a site, a sign, a recur-
rence, whenever we fear the return of the repressed.
Looking within, trying to seek out what is buried,
is a kind of self-eating, or that other thing, an
unleashing of something that might somehow
devour us.

~

People on the long staircase at dusk,
descending, widely spaced. A small group of
students talking animatedly, a businessman,
an elderly woman with a shopping basket –
the couple from the square, part-way up the
middle flight, the only people ascending,
he a few metres ahead of her, studiously not
turning, and she behind, climbing slowly, as if
lost in thought, holding her scarf to her face
against the cold wind.

~

No story is seamless. In every story there are unopened rooms, passageways, shafts leading to other stories, staircases, draughts arriving from dark, cavernous spaces that may be stories the mind is not ready for – between one fact and another, one clause and the next. Even the long story of your life that you have been rehearsing over and over. You walk across a landing and a board breaks beneath you. You pause to let someone catch up and there is a door you had not seen before. You turn around, to tell them, and the person is gone.

Charles saw Chantal only once more, four years later in a house in London. He knocked on the door, she let him in, and they talked in the hallway at the foot of the stairs. He offered her money but she wouldn't take it. He seemed anxious to go, kept looking at his watch and back towards the door, as if there were a car waiting outside.

~

In the Hôtel Ana, a short street from the stairs, on the balcony of a room I had strayed into thinking was my own, two doves were perched close together, so white in the late light with the dark cote behind them that they seemed to be haloed or to burn with a cool, invisible flame. I could not imagine creatures more perfect. Even now. It was as if I had discovered the city's secret, come upon it in a moment of great intimacy, nakedness. One expects fury, horror, the Minotaur, and instead this serenity, this pure, unsuspected light.

~

There are no endings, only sites, only moments of pause or clarity: landings, parapets, points where the stairs pass a window and you can look out briefly before descending – or climbing – into the story again. In one of his dreams he calls Chantal at dusk after a day full of rain. She is driving through hills smoky with oleander. From the top of a rise she has just seen the sun setting, on the far ridges, into a nest of burning cloud, or the light from an ideal city they might soon be reaching.

In another dream he is in Kabul once more, searching for her desperately on the Street of the Carpetsellers, pushing through the crowd with an excited urgency, anticipation rather than fear, watching himself even as he does so with a calm aloofness, as if from a balcony above the stalls. She is nowhere to be seen, he reflects from this vantage, watching himself flailing; nowhere, but an evanescence, a sense of her is everywhere.

CROW THESES

People behave badly. It is not always their fault, and they don't always know it or see it that way. But they do behave badly. It stuns you sometimes, to find that this is happening, that it is going on again, but it is. And the people who behave badly in this way I call the crows. Sometimes it seems that they are landing on you somehow – on your arms, perhaps, or shoulders – and taking small pieces, bites, that other people mightn't see but that leave wounds nonetheless. I know it is unfair to talk about crows in this way. I know that they are just birds, if you can use 'just' there at all, and that it is not the birds' fault that they are the colour they are, or that we humans have this thing about that colour, that blackness, or about the sound they make. But we do have it, and they *are* that colour, they *do* make that sound, and they *have* come to have connotations. Their sound, especially, doesn't help, nor does their habit, in sheep country, of waiting while a ewe is giving birth, to peck out the eyes of the newborn lambs. I'll admit that other birds have raucous cries, and other creatures have habits like that. But not so many of them are black, and they are not crows.

~

The heart, spread out in time, wanders through some strange country – deserts, mountain passes, forests, nameless composite cities, but mostly deserts, often deserts. It seems to me that if there could be a map of such places, to show where the heart had been, to show how, alone, it had fought there, survived there, the crows might begin to understand, might begin to be something other than crows. But men – especially men – do not talk of such things. Only sometimes some event, some predictable occurrence will make them speak, if ever they can find the person to speak to – the deaths of their fathers, their mothers, the deaths or illnesses of their lovers, their wives, their children, or even, sometimes, the devastation that a sudden, unanticipated desire can bring, erupting from a place they had not known existed. Then – in broken sentences, unfinishable sentences – they compare notes and experiences; then the possibilities of a Map begin. A landscape seen as a crow might see it; distances measured 'as the crow flies'.

~

In a film I once saw, of the rituals of a desert tribe in South America – I never did find out what country it was in – a shaman was calling down crows. He was dressed in black, with black wings strapped to his arms, and moving about in a circle, dancing slowly while he chanted, lifting the wings and letting them fall. The sky in the beginning was clear but soon the crows began to arrive, appearing as if out of nowhere. After a time there was a small flock circling about him. When he moved to the centre of the circle he had made, and let his arms fall, they settled on the ground about him and stood there, watching. But what kind of shaman were they watching? The Crow of Loneliness? The Crow of Woundedness? The Crow of Unrelenting Desire?

~

I have a friend who is driven to confess to crimes that he has not committed. That is, he does not *think* he committed them, although he is harried by dreams that seem to point in their direction, of severed limbs, of disembowelment, of people he has known, or seems in these dreams to have known, weeping inconsolably in familiar rooms. It seems impossible to him that these dreams can have nothing to do with him. It seems to him that if he confesses to a crime – any crime, so long as it is a crime that might somehow fit these dreams – these dreams might go away. I would not have thought about crows at all, were it not for the vision, as he described the persistence of these dreams, of the dark wings circling him, flapping about his shoulders.

~

It is not a good day. Incivilities occur; people act as if their mood were all that matters; things happen that shouldn't and it's hard to say why. At last the mail arrives. From one of the envelopes, as I open it, a crow scrambles, all angles and feathers, claws scratching my hands, taking off quickly through the window, circling, returning eventually to perch in a nearby tree. Later, trying to find out about this, I hear crows at the far end of a telephone line. Before I can stop them one or two have come through. For hours they caw about inside my mind. Nothing I can do will silence them.

~

A crow settles on the balcony rail and stares at me through the glass. I go out carefully to talk to it. It does not fly away. I try to explain myself and it listens to me with its crow eyes sceptical, wide. I tell it that the birds I speak of are metaphors only, that I would not presume to speak of crows-in-fact. I tell it that it is not *it* I name, but a part of a system within and about me, in my own human space, and that it is welcome to treat me, as a human, in much the same way. As a symbol of poisoned corn, perhaps, or bad weather, a storm. I tell it that it is a matter of colour alone, a strange prejudice we have. Perhaps that, and what we can only hear as a harshness in its cry. Which it will repeat, as it flies overhead, as if it would not listen to anything we said.

~

To predict the actions of the human, reflects the crow, one must think with the mind of the human. Walking down George Street on an overcast morning, late winter, there is an edginess at the side of things, hovering beside me as I pass a confectioner's, retreating at the recessed windows by the Strand Arcade, disappearing into the stone wall of the GPO, flashing in and out of a blind-spot with a passing car. *Hypocrite*, I want to spit at it, *familiar compound*! Black shoes, black jeans, black jacket, flash of white from my shirt front. Nobody listening.

⁓

The way I see it, which is the way I sometimes imagine others see it also, I have committed many crimes, but they have always been crimes of love. They have always been done *for* it, and *from* it. And I have wanted to say this for a long time now, if only to that other crow, that soft crow, that crow-without-beak-or-claws, that spreads out its wings, to sleep each night on my eyes.

What are the crimes of love, anyway, but fragments of passion broken from their moorings, evidence of a kind of shipwreck? (But what *kind* of ship? Where *was* it? What was its *name*?) Or crows, a flock of them, high in the air, fighting against a wind that no-one can see.

⁓

When I lie down at last, far into the night, the darkness seems to leave me and, retreating to corners, the space under the bed, assumes a more natural shape, eventually filling the room. In the early hours I realise that a crow is there, perched high on the suitcases up on top of the wardrobe, a bit like Poe's raven but also not. Crows are not entirely responsible for their crowness, it is trying to tell me: often, within the mind of the crow, there is a flock of crows circling, driving the crow towards itself. If we could see into the minds of these crows, it is telling me – the crows within the crow – we would find, in many of them, flocks of crows, circling or moving about on the ground there, grown hard and sharp with the warring of the crows inside them.

I stare at the page, thinking of nothing I could readily say. Words, in my abstraction, begin to lose definition. The page begins to exceed its borders, becoming as wide as the sky. A white sky, as it sometimes will be in winter, and in it a flock of crows, in obscure formations. Hieroglyphs. Moving slowly.

We dream of honesty, of openness, but openness can be lacerating. What can be more honest than a crow's cry? What can be more open than a crow's wings as it hovers above a cornfield?

A.

Over and again one comes to the City, like the death of one's father, one's mother, worst love, the worst or the greatest pleasure, a thing one can never adequately write about although one tries all one's life, over and again shuffling the disparate fragments knowing that somehow they belong together, never finding the key – a place exotic and unapproachable, though time after time one comes to its gates and stares inward, through the dark, weathered timber, at the steady weight of sunlight, the slow, ordinary movements of the ordinary, familiar people on the streets within, the dogs, camels, donkeys, sheep, and the coloured awnings of the stalls, the goods being taken to and from market.

They say that we carry deep within us a memory of all the places we have ever lived, of all the spaces that have made us their familiar, and that this memory in its turn shapes and colours the places we afterwards might dwell, but when was it that we all – that I – first entered A.?

There are many ways of getting there. One of them is simply to set out and to keep moving until you find it. Another is to gather together all of those moments from your life so far when you have come across a site or smell or taste or thing which you have seemed to know intimately, but for which intimacy you could find no explanation, and to accept them as glimpses, as the beginnings of A. Another, of course, is to record your dreams. Still another is simply to look within – at your mind, your heart, your small daily habits, the way you shape your sentences – and to find out what kind of place it is you have hidden there. Even if that is only the faintest sketch of a place, the merest trace. Even if all that remains is the initial, the letter only in the alphabet of the mind, the lofty arch of it, that pointed attic space, the broad, hearthed room beneath it would return us to the time that gave it origin, no mere trick of rhetoric, no sleight of text, but the first letter, the beginning of all. One sees pictures of an ancient city of the Sahara, perhaps, or Kazakhstan, and says Yes, that is it. One sees a painting of Innsbruck – the cobbled streets, the outdoor market, the spires, the turreted roofs – and knows it is there too, a confluence of our deepest images and desire, a place every heart, every mind, every unconscious turn of the body somehow unknowingly knows, shaped no more by experience than by the first touch of the lip on the mother's breast, the first glimpse of light, the first searing breath of air in the infant's lungs, and all the cognates of these things: the first colour, the first word, the first knowledge of that other – that father – who also made one.

Yet A. is also distinctive, also entirely one's own. There is something arbitrary even in the selection of the initial, although also not. The letter itself occurs in word after word, as if to remind us that the beginning is always with us. But that is not why I have chosen it, if in fact I have had choice at all. I call it A., I sometimes think, because it is a city like Alexandria, or rather, since I have never been to Alexandria, what I have imagined that city to be like, from all the images I have seen of it, all the things I have read. If this makes it sound as if A. is also something in the mind, a kind of process of thought, then well and good, since any city must also be such a thing. I don't only mean the way we carry deep in our minds the maps and shapes and atmospheres of the earliest cities of our experience, so that any subsequent city is also in some part these cities, too, since it is perceived by the mind itself that these cities first taught to see, although I do also mean this.

There is, let us say, a harbour in A., but you need not live on the harbour. There are also hills behind the city, but you need not live amongst them. Within the perpetual alternation of the dry heat and the heavy winter rains (winter? is it ever winter there?) – in the palm-shaded courtyards, the narrow alleys behind the great central market, the airconditioned rooms of the luxury hotels – there is a considerable variety of climates and weathers, but you need not experience them. Doubtless those who live and work about the harbour think of A. as a harbour city, just as those who work high up in the hill mines think of the harbour as serving them, or those who live in the dry, flat reaches on the desert's edge think of A. as an oasis from the heat and sand, a place at the end of a trade route, controlled by transactions that neither the harbour nor the miners consider. A. is all of these things, a different city for everyone who reaches it, a different memory for everyone who leaves.

In a system reflecting and perhaps integral to all of these things, A. is governed, unobtrusively, sometimes almost tacitly, by an assembly of poets and philosophers – which is to say that it is hardly governed at all, in the usual way of arrangements for garbage collection, approval of roads, provision for municipal taxes (these things are left, as perhaps they should be, to administrators), but governed nonetheless, impalpably yet almost utterly. The assembly meets annually, for anything from a few days to two weeks or more, in a large hall built for the purpose almost eleven centuries ago, a building with a great cupola and high, unglazed openings so arranged as to let the dusty light fall naturally on the floor beneath it into a circle the size of which has always determined the size of the assembly. It might hold fifty or sixty quite comfortably – somewhat more if the occasion demands – but in fact there are rarely more than a dozen. I call them poets and philosophers, although these terms, loose enough in themselves, only approximate the nature and function of the legislation produced here, and might belie the very real sense in which these people are self-selected.

It is not unusual to find amongst the assembly a banker, say, or a midwife, a nurse, a priest, a housewife, a cooper or a digger of drains, each of whom has found themselves called by what they themselves have construed, or perhaps it is simply *realised*, to be the poet or philosopher within.

In the shadowed places far below the cupola, between the columns about the lighted circle, people gather to listen to the proceedings, almost always in silence but for an occasional murmur of approval, puzzlement or dismay. Sometimes these people are many – again it depends upon the issue – and sometimes only a few, but it is often from these shadows that a new member of the assembly comes, having attended perhaps for a number of years, sitting or standing outside the circle, and learnt, and thought, and found at last the confidence or need to step out. At which time, it should be said, they are never questioned, for this is the manner in which so many of those already there have also arrived. There is no romance in the work, no *kudos*, no power that one can readily utilise or see, no statesmanlike name to be made since names are so rarely carried beyond the confines of the hall. It is not for these reasons that people step forward.

Rather, it is that their minds have been caught up in an ancient and intricate discussion, the rules and assumptions of which, contained always within the collective consciousness of the assembly, have passed down from generation to generation for over a thousand years. If the assembly is always open to the newcomer – and there are, as I have already intimated, those who enter the circle for only one meeting, or who come and go almost without notice – it is always guided by its elders whose minds, over the years, have become vast repositories of the discussions that have passed.

The first and strongest of these rules, determining the fate and course of any new subject or idea, is that no such thing may be ventured upon without preface or precedent within the discussions of the assembly itself. All things must connect. Every new idea must be demonstrated to have its seed or origin in a previous idea; every new subject must begin in a subject somewhere before it; any new thought must be taken to the venerable river of thought that has run down, in this manner, through the ages. Thus the discourse itself can be seen to determine its own paths, accepting or rejecting what is brought to it by force of what it has accepted or rejected before. The poets, the philosophers who would take part in the government of the city have freedom, but only within the parameters of what the past will allow.

This is not always as confining as it might at first appear. Individual poets or philosophers wishing to introduce new matters of concern need not themselves present the precedents required, but may call upon the collective memory. If precedent exists, one or another of the elders will find it. Nor, intriguingly, is this the sole recourse. Now and again, some say, an idea is raised that through sheer force of intellect or circumstance cannot very easily be rejected, although it appears that no precedent can be found. In which case something else may happen. A few days may pass in which the matter is not mentioned; sometimes a full year passes, or more; and then someone – it is usually but not always the most senior of the elders – will raise the matter again, having thought carefully meanwhile, and having remembered, now, something which had at first slipped their mind. A thing said by one of those who had attended only one meeting, many years ago now – probably no-one else would remember – the pertinence of which has taken some time to make itself clear. And a name will be given, or some personal detail, for such is the way these things must be. And then the elder will spell out an idea or formula, carefully constructed so as to provide a bridge between the ancient discourse and the new idea whose worth had proved so irresistible. And at this point, jogged by this forgotten link, convinced by its logic, its rightness, others will begin to recall. So that, given force enough of desire, a new idea can create its own precedent, the present augment the past, an old man – so the cynics say – bring into being someone who had never existed.

It's this that I have been wanting to tell you about, the invention. I had wondered all along why there were poets as well as philosophers, but in the light of A. it now seems so clear, and that in reality there is little difference, or that it is a difference only in degree; that the ancient battle between the poets and philosophers is a battle of the same. That now and again the philosophers need the poets to cover their traces, or to imagine the way that, imagined, becomes the way. And that without them it might not be the burning possibility that in the core of every one of us it is.

This, and the ancient custom of the place, long abandoned, of the voluntary blinding and sequestrating of elders in memory of one of the earliest and most venerable of them – he who is claimed to have founded the city, and to have been blind from birth – so that thereafter they could not see the city they were asked to talk about, but only hold it in their minds, as perhaps did that first founder, never quite letting the actual city of A. eclipse the city he pursued, through all his long eldership, so ardently in his mind.

Sometimes, in the midst of an assembly, like a reminder of something the poets and philosophers can never quite put their finger on, one of the doves or pigeons with which the streets and the eaves of the city abound will get in through a high window space and flap about in the great dome above them. People, at these times, wonder how it will ever get out, and fight the temptation to run about after it, trying to capture it or usher it through one of the lower doors, but somehow always it escapes, as often by going up and into the middle darkness as by flying back down, of its own accord, through one of the open spaces, as if there are secret openings there that no-one could reach even if they wanted to.

THE LIGHTHOUSE KEEPER'S DREAM

for Pat Ricketts

A lighthouse keeper dreams that he is a man dreaming that he is the keeper of a lighthouse. The lighthouse in the dream of the man in the lighthouse keeper's dream is not the lighthouse that the lighthouse keeper is in fact the keeper of. The lighthouse keeper's lighthouse is on the tip of a headland on a temperate southern coastline, facing eastward, warmed half the year by currents coming down from the distant tropics and, in the rest, when the warm currents move further offshore, chilled by currents coming north from the distant polar seas. In almost every season, on calmer days, and there are many of these, dolphins come to play in the waves that wash the rocks at the foot of the low cliff upon which the lighthouse stands. The lighthouse keeper's lighthouse is connected to a nearby highway by a long, winding road through a rainforest. Every morning and early evening, if it is not raining and there is no wind, the lighthouse keeper can hear the calls of birds – kookaburras mainly, but also parrots, currawongs, butcherbirds, and sometimes even a whipbird or a bellbird – drifting across the grassy clearing that separates the lighthouse from the edge of the forest. A few kilometres from the point where the forest meets the highway is a small fishing town to which the lighthouse keeper can go, when there is someone to relieve him, to shop, or visit friends, drink at the local pub, or see a movie at the local cinema. At other times, when he cannot go into the town himself, he can telephone to almost any of the local businesses and have them deliver whatever it may be that he requires.

Although exposed on the headland and visible from twenty kilometres or more along the coast to the north and south of it, the lighthouse keeper's lighthouse is not often buffeted by storms, and any heavy seas that hit the coast play themselves out more or less harmlessly upon the rocky base of the cliff. Only rarely, if there is a strong wind accompanying them, does spray from the waves reach high enough to be felt by someone standing at the base of the lighthouse itself. Beside the squat white tower of the lighthouse are two small cottages, built closely side by side. The lighthouse keeper lives in one of these; the other, now empty, was for the assistant keeper and his family, when there was an assistant keeper, before the lighthouse was automated to the extent that it now is. And behind the cottages, some fifty metres further away, towards the other side of the headland, in a small cleared space amongst the low scrub, is a graveyard in which are buried two of the previous keepers of the lighthouse, two assistant keepers, with various members of their families, and members of the families of other keepers and assistant keepers of the light.

The lighthouse dreamt of by the man in the lighthouse keeper's dream, on the other hand, is so isolated and so constantly assailed by the heaving of the sea that it is almost inconceivable that it exist at all. Four kilometres from the coast, built on the westernmost of the very rocks it warns passing vessels away from, the techniques, let alone the bravery, of those who constructed it have been a source of awe to all who have subsequently set eyes upon it. It seems as if the sea in this place can never have rested, never have stayed calm long enough for the first stones to be set, the first foundations to be laid, and yet the lighthouse has stood and warned sailors from its dangerous shoal for almost two hundred years. In one part of his dream the man of whom the lighthouse keeper dreams sees the keeper of this light – himself? and yet how could it be? – standing in the arched doorway set into the foot of the lighthouse, holding onto a handrail, looking up to where the dreamer looks at him. A wave half as high as the lighthouse itself – a wave of almost inconceivable force and mass – is about to crash upon it from the other side. The base of the lighthouse is at this moment like a tunnel, an alcove between monstrous walls of sea. It seems incredible that the lighthouse keeper is standing there. It seems incredible that he will survive, incredible that he will not be washed away.

The lighthouse keeper's life – the life of the lighthouse keeper who dreams of the man who dreams that he is a lighthouse keeper – is a lonely life, by most standards, but he is a solitary man by nature, and resourceful, and his loneliness is mitigated by the fact that he can go into the town now and again, and by the number of people who drive in along the forest road, in all but the worst weather, to visit the lighthouse and take in its marvellous view. Less than one hundred metres to the north of the lighthouse itself there is a path from the cliff-top to a small, sheltered beach below. On any warm, calm day, if he is unable or disinclined to sleep, the lighthouse keeper can go down to this beach to swim or to sunbathe out of sight of the lighthouse and any visitors who might come to it, or can double back to have his afternoon tea upon a rock ledge almost directly below the lighthouse.

The life of the lighthouse keeper in the dream of the man in the lighthouse keeper's dream is very different. Although by any measure he is almost certainly more resourceful and more solitary by nature than the lighthouse keeper who dreams of the man who dreams of him, his loneliness is often a deep and cold and aching thing, that seems to penetrate almost everything he touches or that touches him – the mug into which he pours his evening coffee (for like most lighthouse keepers he sleeps by day, works through the night), the table upon which he eats his meals, the circular iron stairway to the prism, far above where he sleeps, the cramped alcove where he has his bed, the bed itself, the cold light that filters down to him in the morning as he undresses and lies down there.

From the top of his lighthouse the lighthouse keeper looks out, for much of the time, upon calm seas and a clear view to the eastern horizon. The lighthouse keeper in the dream of the man in the lighthouse keeper's dream, however, looks out on fury, king waves that sometimes seem as if they will douse his light, snap the strong tower of the lighthouse as if it were made of matchwood. There are days aplenty when he can see the western horizon, though very often it is jagged with storm. There are many days more when the mist or fog closes in and he must forgo anything but the most broken sleep in order to maintain the long, mournful groans of the horn that, night and day in such weather, must try to do the job of the light that cannot be seen. Although sometimes, when the ocean has taken on an eerie grey calm, a herd of sea lions has been known to appear almost a kilometre directly westward, and whales that, could they speak, might bring news of one lighthouse to the other, the paradox of this man's situation is that the ocean which surrounds him is in so many ways unreachable, untouchable. No dolphins come to play by the treacherous rocks, no swimming or sunbathing is possible, no fishing conceivable in the seething water.

Nor are there graves, in this dream of the man in the lighthouse keeper's dream. Where would one put them? The ocean itself is a grave. Seven men were washed to their deaths in the building of the lighthouse in this man's dream – the tragedies had once been news throughout the country – and the raging ocean swallowed them all, so that as he looks out at the relentless heaving of the deep, blue-black water, it seems to him, the lighthouse keeper in the dream of the man in the lighthouse keeper's dream, as if he is looking out at the very death that he is trying so hard to save people from.

On the calmest days, in this man's dream, and only on the calmest days, a supply boat is able to land and deliver fuel and provisions and instructions from the Maritime Services Board, although as often as not the captain of the supply boat will determine that the risk of landing is too great and will choose instead to shoot a line to the lighthouse keeper – often, himself protected by a safety-rope, he has to fish this out with a grappling hook from one of the rocks at the lighthouse's base – and deliver his provisions by way of a basket and pulley, so that beyond what can be shouted through the wind over the thirty metres between the vessel and the lighthouse, his human communication is limited to radio frequencies and the barely audible static-laden telegraphy of the maritime traffic.

Waking from his dream – it is a recurrent dream that has been a part of his life since his first year at the lighthouse – the keeper always wonders why the man in his dream should find himself dreaming of such a lighthouse and such an existence. What it might be, deep within each of them – for he knows that everything in every dream is in some way an extension of the dreamer – that is so lonely, so isolated, so beleaguered, that it chooses for itself this place, this life, sending out messages that are no more than glimmers or bars of light, or repetitions of the one deep, mournful note, warning people, on vessels that he cannot see, of the dangers, the perils of approaching too near.

THE DEAD

Angels, they say, don't know whether it is the living they are moving among, or the dead …
'First Elegy', R.M. Rilke, trans. Stephen Mitchell

Mid-winter sunrise, deep vermilion, etched against the dark towers, cold and fiery dawn-ball of godspeech, horns like lost geese in the depths below. Traffic gropes along streets not yet quite drained of night. On the bed beside me a woman is weeping for the waste of life. Hers. Mine. Or perhaps for some other thing entirely.

It is only later that I see them, naked like myself but out there on the tops of buildings, leaning against chimneys or airducts or standing right at the prows, like young midshipmen. Some vast invisible sea.

When I wake again it is broad, cold day. Buildings have recovered their colours. The herds of taxis bank and flow with the lights. Where there might have been something else there now are only doves, or white pigeons, coasting between the rooftops, high over the numbered avenues, beaks closed hard against the light.

~

At 6.45 a.m. there was a Moroccan woman singing somewhere below, her voice rising strong and confident from the stairwell. At first I thought it was a record, a nightclub, but at that hour? And then, at seven, the strangest sound from above, beyond, or even from within the building itself, a courtyard I haven't yet seen. Like the cooing of pigeons, greatly amplified, or some much larger bird being fed. (Geese. Could it have been the geese again, echoing up some atrium?)

And for almost an hour now there have been sounds of water, baths being run, ablutions, a child's voice far below chattering in a language I don't understand, the city itself at last breaking through. Motors running. Doors slamming. A distant siren. Soon there will be the noisy garbage collection, the collection of rubble from the work down the street. Soon the woman coming to work in the Institute of Beauty, with her yapping dog …

~

Out for air after a whole day's rain we walk to the park on the boulevard, returning along the street by the cemetery. The high roofs of the dead are just visible over the long, straight walls, some of them with their windows open, catching the last light. I think about them sitting there, in their upper storeys, with their hands on the sill, their mouths and eyes gaping, absorbing whatever they can from the thin, buttery sun.

~

Just before 6 a.m. in Room 4 of the Hotel
Guerrini, for a couple of hours now awake and
yet hearing nothing – a complete absence of cars,
as if we were out in the country. Only the occasional person, very late or early, crossing the square
outside. At one point a girl's laughter, at another
the sound of snoring from the next room. And
the sound of her sleeping. A few moments before
I rose I actually heard her dreaming, her breathing
getting suddenly deeper and more rapid as she fled
something or ran after it down one of the lanes or
alleyways, deep in the ancient city of the mind.
And then, for a few minutes, the sound of birds.
At breakfast I asked her what it had been, but she
was confused, remembered nothing, did not know
what I was asking.

*

Walking down a dark street late at night we pass
a fragment of the old city walls. I realise that the
City of the Dead is also walled, its perimeters still
intact and that in other ways too it is, as in this,
a replica of the city about it. For the City of the
Dead is also divided into sectors and has its grand
avenues and narrow back lanes, its parks and
public spaces: there is the Avenue A, the Avenue T,
the Boulevard N; there are C Street and L Street.
So that the dead have their own, particular
addresses. So that there are some neighbourhoods
more sought after than others. So that there is an
English quarter, a Jewish quarter, a Chinese. At

the gatehouse I ask for the poet V and am told that he is on rue D, number 49, just a few doors down from the fountain.

~

You would think all the small birds in this place had already been trapped and eaten by the peasants, but that is another country, the official one, the one of rumour. Here everything is birds and bells, small streets, passageways, arches, unexpected stairways and issuings. It seems like a model of the heart somehow, although every time I try to explain this the threads slip away. There is a clock in a bell tower that is thirty minutes behind, and so rings out the strangest hours, one peal for the third quarter, three for the first one, two for the hour, one, nine or ten or twelve for the half-hour later. There is another that rings out the correct hours, but are they the correct hours truly? We are in different territory. Every day you feel another life waiting. Every day you feel you could step off the edge.

~

We compare our nights. No-one sleeps well. No-one really tells the truth of them. Jealous for what the night means to us, we are clutching at our small parcels of dark, holding them back from the light. We keep our shutters closed far into the morning, long after the sounds have begun outside. When we

open them at last the day is thunderous, the sound
and the colour blaze through in a wild confusion.

~

*The first time I woke I heard rain approaching over
the roofs, gently at first but then hard and driving
overhead, tailing off again as quickly as it came,
leaving the night clean. The second time light was
beginning to filter through the half-open shutters.
Some of it had got in already and was wrapping
itself about this object and that, making the shapes
of them clear. I thought I saw a lone tongue dart in,
one of the tiny tongues of the dawn birds, or it may
have been a lone ray of gold, shining for an instant
on the surface of an urn before the earthly matter
swallowed it.*

~

Is it death in us, or are we waiting, in a kind of
hibernation, to wake into some new state, some
different spring?

Is that what we came here for, to wander about
in the shadowy streets of ourselves, bear witness to
them, in an alarm or amazement we can do little
to explain or control?

~

A rat swims over the fine plate of Isabella d'Este,
making for the beard of green algae growing from

her brother's hand. Down the street three *putti*, smiling over a scene now gone, show the same vapid delight as the cloud they ride goes slowly under. The City is half below water. The builders knew this would happen. Perhaps, thinking of lost Atlantis, they even planned it so. Boats scrape against the ground-floor lintels, gondolas are garaged over sunken dining rooms. Whatever may be left in the cellars far below now rests in inaccessible silence. No light enters there. Where once guests gathered at the foot of great staircases, amongst frescoes of Diana or the Princes of Umbria, no-one, not even if they have just dropped the most valuable jewel, attempts to dive into the polluted shadow. At night people wake and hear the water somewhere beneath them, and wonder if they have woken at all, if it isn't the mind that is under flood, if they don't spend half their lives under its waters.

~

In some paintings it is not a halo or nimbus but rays of gold or golden arrows descending from the sky, piercing now a bird, now a child, now a man or, more often, a woman, in all the configurations of Annunciation. In the left-hand panel of 'The Penitence of St Jerome' by Joachim Patinir the rays pour like a bizarre golden beard from about the cloud-enshrouded mouth of God, shooting down at first into a dove and then to St John who baptises the semi-naked Christ in a river that has also commenced in the clouds, the mind and the eye being gathered, herded by these things, so that later, in a church we had mistaken for the Pantheon, how could we be surprised to find, in a corner, behind protective glass, a painting of the Pentecost and golden tongues drifting down through the air, a small swarm or squadron, towards the waiting mouths of the apostles?

~

In the City of Ruins it is the unexpected eruptions of life that we look for, a bright carpet of lawn amongst the broken columns and buckling paving of a cloister, a tree burgeoning with lemons at the end of a barren stone alley, a huge-speared succulent like a still green fountain in a shaft of light amongst the crumbled mosaics and desecrated frescoes, living water bubbling from an ancient fountain. Once a child, following with his younger brother his parents as they conversed fluently with a guide in the strange language of this place, turned to me and, looking openly, spoke in my own tongue, the one clear, intimate word of greeting, as if he knew me and there were some treasured secret between us. All afternoon his strange beauty haunted the stone, sounds that might have been their muffled voices leading me deeper and deeper into the dry, hot maze of that place, investing it with unexpected and implausible desire.

~

Although there have been countless reports about the city and the various cities within it, there appears to have been none about that city which is made up of reports of itself – as Venice, say, is a confluence of the texts that have been written about it; the Venice inhabited – as Alexandria is inhabited, as London is, as Sydney, as Paris – by people who have read the texts written about it and who, when they look at the city about them, see the city those authors have written about, and try to live as they imagine the people in those texts might have lived.

The City *is* what the City *was*. If we are taught to see by the stories we see or hear or read, if our vision is always the product of texts – the texts we have seen, and those seen by those who have written what we have seen – then the City that *is* is a hole, an absence, a possibility, beyond us, as we ourselves are, as our friends are, our lovers. An edge, which now and again we think we glimpse through accident, irruption, exposure.

~

In the poet's house there was an alcove in a small recessed area off the entrance hall, an alcove inside an alcove. This alcove, the smaller one – the alcove within the alcove – was in fact a painting of a woman in a chapel or further alcove, a tall woman in a dress of vivid red, her arms outstretched so that the pale grey shawl she also wore formed a kind of tent over the space beneath her. In this space were several people – other women, priests, burghers of a town (such was my explanation of the waves about them) somewhere by the sea. Many of them – not all, since some appeared to have turned their faces to the waves – were looking up with expressions of quiet adoration to her own absorbed and meditative face. She was their Nurse, their Virgin, the young, strong, infinitely caring Mother they remembered from the time when they were children, before the lines entered her face and her neck bowed, before her hair thinned and turned grey. Suspended on the wall as she was, her arms wide apart and the shawl so like a canopy about her, she was fixed in the one place and yet, every time I looked towards her – for she could be seen through the archway from the table where I sat with the poet, eating a pasta with a sauce of cheese and pancetta and eggs, and drinking a fine Amarone – she seemed also to be rising, a phenomenon, a tension, a paradox which, sitting there so attently, my physical relation to it never changing, I could only explain as the room itself moving with her, and all of us – the woman, the poet, his daughters, myself – slowly rising from the earth.

~

There was a moment, she once told me, when it seemed she had lived utterly, when it had felt as if she glimpsed into the *reality* of things, so that ever since, when a similar moment occurred, she felt that she should collect it and place it with others, as if they might all belong to some different place, the true place, the place of which all these places were dreaming ...

~

It was not the City; none of them was; but when, in the Campo de' Fiori, the birds lifted off the shoulders of the statue of Giordano Bruno (it was just sunset, and the last rays of light were disappearing over the roofs of the houses) their beaks were open – this is the point: their beaks were open in a farewell cry and the light, the very last of it, caught for a merest fragment of a second in this open space, breaking into minute sun-burrs, tiny radiant clusters, in the very moment of its vanishing.

~

Walking back from the City of the Dead we passed many others walking in the direction opposite to our own, but saw them with a doubt we had not thought of as we came. Were these people, as we had done an hour earlier, heading out for a Sunday stroll, or were they returning? And which city were they returning to? Which of us were the living and which the dead?

~

In the city the darkness is relative: you enter the street, late at night, from a well-lighted room, or simply turn off the light within that room, or carry a light out-of-doors before you, and the darkness can seem almost total until your eyes adjust, until shapes, in a gradual thinning of the darkness, begin to reappear in what might best be thought of not as night, but as a ghost or shadow of the day, the day that exists, even when day is not there, the strange light, the *between* light, that is not creating the darkness by its own being.

~

In the Hotel Guerrini I dream again of water, great waves of ocean from beyond the horizon moving inexorably towards the rocks and the low, city cliffs upon which we stand, breaking at last at the harbour's mouth, washing so high over the beach and the breakwater that we must run skipping, leaping backwards to avoid them. A terrible storm is coming, they say, and we must retreat to the house of our friends, to wait in the great hall, murmuring amongst ourselves, a low fire struggling in the huge grate, watching for a sign of the gale's passing, the sound of birds perhaps, or light at a battened window.

What is it about? they ask me. What does it mean? Do I know that the City is about to be swept away? And there is, after all, only so much I can show them. Only this ...

TEN SHORT PIECES

ALCHEMY

After much experimentation, many failed attempts, the alchemist has succeeded, at least with one part of the process. Laying out, at dusk, in grassy places, vast sheets of a specially woven fabric – well-oiled, dark-proof – he finds that at dawn he is able to gather the condensed night in pannikins. Carefully distilling the cloudy liquid in alembics specifically created for the task, he then distributes the rich, black essence into small bottles for his agents to peddle to scholars, artists, clerics and scribes. These, in their turn, with the aid of trimmed goose feathers, sable brushes, or small sticks tipped with a kind of metal claw, tease out the substance carefully into fine, horizontal webs on sheets of calfskin or paper which then they let dry before making available to others who, inspecting them closely, become peculiarly affected, feeling a sort of distilled, ineffable darkness or numbness entering their veins, the most likely and immediate consequences of which are insomnia, or a tendency towards drunkenness, and wandering about late at night, barefooted in grassy places, like grieving cattle, leaving a strange web behind them in the dew.

A Piece of Sheepsong

Very often, when I think of myself writing, I have in my mind
an image of a man at a table in a workshop, in a small pool of
light. He may be making a shoe, he may be repairing a watch, he
may be an artist, or an artist's artisan, working on an engraving.
What precisely he is doing does not matter very much, because
in my mind he is also, as he cuts a sliver of leather, slips a small
cog into place, or cross-hatches a tiny area of shadow, a writer,
carefully choosing the words, shaping the phrases, paring his
thoughts to their elements, saying, over and over, what lines
he has in the hope that one of these lines will run on, will spill
over into something he has not yet imagined – now and again
reaching, where a shoemaker might reach for an awl or a watch-
maker for a tiny spring, into a small tool cabinet on the table
beside him for a piece of sheepsong or the end of a shower of
rain, an owl.

Process

It is a process. A contingent of police and officials raid an
Immigration Detention Centre to arrest the ringleaders of a
recent disturbance at the facility. These ringleaders are moved
to a further site of detention, at an undisclosed location. Back
at the Detention Centre, amongst those who had been led by
these ringleaders, there is disquiet at this turn of events. New
leaders emerge. New detainees arrive by boat or bus from
where they have been apprehended trying to enter the country

illegally. A new disturbance occurs, the ringleaders are arrested in a second raid and taken to swell the ranks of those taken away after the original disturbance. Discontent – there has never been anything but discontent – mounts. Ringleaders emerge to lead the ringleaders. A wild disturbance breaks out. Alarmed, police and immigration officials stage a raid on the undisclosed location, arresting the ringleaders, whom they take to a further undisclosed location …

A Short Allegory

A writer comes back to a paragraph he has written some years before, hoping he can take up its thread but finding he cannot. It is a story, of course, but the story does not exist – or rather, exists, for here is the trace – but he is no longer able to follow it. A man, it seems, has walked deeper and deeper into the jungle of his lover's eyes – or perhaps it is only his own – leaving behind only this fragment, like a pencil, a cigarette lighter, a box of matches he might have forgotten, a last few sentences scrawled hastily to a friend only moments before taking his first steps into the giant trees, following something he has glimpsed there and, so great has been his haste to follow it, he has not had the time to describe it for us.

'Imagine', the paragraph begins 'a jungle consisting not of trees, vines, mosses, flowers, but of towering sentences, dense paragraphs, referents, predicates intertwined and almost impenetrable, here and there, in small clearings, great-flowering words, phrases newly sprung from the damp ground starting to twine, even as one watches them, about the thick trunks or ground-touching limbs or, far above, leaning out from one sentence to another, giving themselves into the strange, separate world of the thickening canopy, the great cope of the text. Imagine the colours and exotic scents here. Imagine the snakes that lie in these vines, the birds that now and again flash suddenly from one sentence to another. Imagine – for this is what you do – the unimagined tribe that has never before had contact with your own civilisation, and that moment when, breaking through a veil of green words, you catch your first glimpse of brown limbs, black hair and a bright bird, breaking from the high phrases, shrieks, a piercing cry that goes out over the whole forest as if to register the end of everything.'

A Time of Strangers

… So it was, anyway, that we entered a time of strangers. It was hard to know how it had come about. Perhaps all that can be confidently said is that we must have had a great need of them, or – could this be possible? – they as greatly and suddenly a need of us. We found ourselves painting them, writing them. We found ourselves talking about them. We found that we had begun to dream of them. It was as if we had, many of us, been given suddenly, inexplicably, enchanted spectacles, wonderful glasses, that enabled us to see what had been invisible before, or that somewhere about us, within us, a barrier, a wall, a distance had broken down and beings were able to circulate among us that had been kept away longer than any of us could know. It is hard to say when the visions, the sense of their presences began, and for some time those of us who had seen or felt them had kept them to themselves, afraid that others would not understand, fearing – in fact certain, so great had become our loneliness – that these things could only be happening to ourselves alone. Now, after longer reflection – given what we have come to know – there may be those among us who are prepared to allow a kind of mass hysteria, a contagious suggestion, as if, as with all ideas whose times have come, there had been a need for the idea of them, and that idea itself had called them into being. (Do you see there the circles in my own thought, the specious argument? But I am convinced that the very thing that propels it, that turns it in upon itself despite all sense of reason or proportion, is typical of the things that revealed them to us in the first place.) Perhaps at last all that we can say is that the name, the thought of such creatures, had come again to us, to supply the questions, the vacuums, the shadows that beauty or wonder or fear had begun so urgently to set abroad. For we had tried all else – the confidence, the encyclopaedic knowledges, the cynicism – and perhaps it was that, the exhaustion, the loss of direction, the listlessness, that created the platform for their arrival, if arrival it was and not, as at other times it seemed, a sudden, inexplicable thickening of the atmosphere about us, as if what one day had been mere air had the next become inhabited, had taken on not only sinew, motion, but visage, character, identity as familiar as it was strange, as strange as it was hauntingly familiar. For although in our painting or our writing we had transformed them, in actual appearance they were almost always like ourselves – but for the cleanliness of line, the distinctive inner light that pearled every feature, the aura about them of a pale, bruising fire (once, in November, I held a face in my hands: I hoped the scent, the cool white burning on my palms would last forever).

It was almost the end of the world, that was the thing. At least, there were more and more of us who found ourselves close to believing it. Air was running out, space was running out, imagination was running out, and so many of us had been wrought by this to such a frenetic pace that a kind of self-destruction seemed imminent and almost logical. We had given up resisting. We had given up hoping. We had given up trying to explain. We had even stopped posturing, had even stopped thinking there was something we should say. And in that torpor had found a strange relaxation, a lightening, even a kind of undesperate, effortless joy in the irresistible insanities of the heart. And then these beings. As if – but not actually? – from behind doorways, from the arms of our chairs, from the pillows beside us, rounding corners in front of us or falling into step beside us, staring at us from bus seats, looking up from desks or turning towards us in crowds with such intimate expressions, *opennesses*, a recognition that seemed to go through us, to penetrate immediately the heart of us, so that it was all that we could do to hold back from rising and, leaving our bags, stepping off from the bus, walking into the crowd to follow them. Not that they were all golden, all beings of light or beauty, for there were the darker ones, too, creatures of garbage, creatures of stone, bleak creatures, creatures of hate, creatures of emptiness, weakening creatures, creatures of drowning (and so many did, so many drowned).

What they were, what it was that had so fertilised the seed-beds of our desire to create such an astonishing blossoming, to cause so exotic and alluring a mould upon our minds and spirits is hard enough to say, but harder still, in so many ways, is it to say why it was that they left. What had we said? What rule, what law had we broken? Was it the hope itself that somehow, in all that, began again, as if all such beings can only be beings of hopelessness? Was it that tiny sprout of green confidence, there amongst the asphalt grey? All that can be said is that, slowly, reluctantly, we came back to ourselves, and were now somewhat embarrassed by what had been, by what we had claimed to see, and had now to brace ourselves, as someone must recompose themselves after great laughter or unbounded sorrow, unbounded passion, and prepare themselves for the street, the people in the next room, relegating these delicate and extraordinary creatures – that *had* kissed us, that *had* taken our faces in their hands, that *had* come to the place just at the centre of our breastbone and undone the button there, and pushed their soft and exquisite tongues into the very secret and melting hearts of us, or passed, momentarily, their hot, intoxicating breath about our ears, or left about our necks and throats the kisses like clustered grapes with the mist of dawn still on them – again to the realm of the unthinkable. What *had* we said, what *had* we done? Was it, perhaps, as simple, and as complicated, as a single word, a word which, having long forgotten it, we uttered too often and too loudly in our delight, our uncontainable relief at so suddenly, so unexpectedly finding it again, a word that, even as I write of them, I can hardly – dare I? – bring myself to say?

In the Centre of the World

A moon has appeared in a tree. High up among the leaves and branches, yet visible from every direction, almost as if the leaves and the branches were not there at all. Not the real moon, which is still shining brightly above, but a small, perfect, different moon, right in the middle, silvery white with most of its craters intact, so like the real moon that it seems wrong to say it isn't real also.

Someone from the village has found it and alerted others, and now a small crowd has gathered. Almost everyone is there. Some people try to reach it using ladders and rakes, but it is so high up that when they step into the tree to take hold of it the thin upper branches bend too much, or start to break beneath their weight. Some – the very lightest, the best climbers, the children – can actually touch it, but only just, with the tips of their fingers, and say that it feels like a small, wet, sandy rock at midnight, with the shine of the other moon on it. Others bring torches, as if light from something else might somehow explain it. Still others throw stones and pine cones and clods of earth, as always some people will do. But everything bounces right off it with a quiet and solid, non-metallic sound – the moon is hardly affected – and pretty soon they simply stand and stare like everyone else. A moon, a perfect moon, way up in the middle of a tree, in the centre of a farmer's field, in what now, suddenly, unexpectedly, seems like it must, after all, be the centre of the world.

In the morning it is gone, of course, as all moons are. But then, everybody agrees, it was a small, thin, thumbnail moon, as all moons also are, always, on the night before they disappear.

VIERGE OUVRANTE

A woman gives birth to death while a man stands watching – after all, he is the father, and what else can he do, his own death grown so large inside him, almost ready to be born?

THE NET

High in the night sky over a country far below the equator the moon is casting great swathes of silver light into the emptiness about it. As they near the earth, transected by the high, thin tessellations of the evening cloud, they appear to turn into the kind of net that fishermen use to pull in sardines or mackerel from the bright night waters of the Mediterranean, or that natives might have employed, some hours earlier, in the broad, flat waters of a moonlit bay off an island in the South Pacific.

Far below, a man is standing on a balcony, staring upwards, thinking of nothing but the moon's astonishing brightness – the way, passing through a shoal of cloud that stretches away to the invisible horizon, it is as if the moon's light were rising towards him from the bottom of a shallow sea. A corner of the net has entered his eyes. As might have been predicted, and without the aid of his actual hands – in fact without his being conscious of this at all – the mind of the man, arm over arm, is hauling in the bright fish of the moon.

A TURKISH HEAD

The family of a veteran of the Gallipoli campaign, deceased at last at the age of one hundred and three, visit his house in Bendigo – it has been abandoned for years – and find in the potting shed, amongst his pieces of broken furniture and garden implements and suitcases full of old photograph albums and pianola rolls and 78 rpm records, a wooden box containing the severed head of a Turkish soldier, preserved as if mummified. The head is distorted and a dark unnatural brown, but still recognisable, with its teeth and moustache intact and a bullet-hole just above the right eye. After a great deal of debate and a few discreet and embarrassed phone calls the granddaughter finally persuades the family to give the relic up to the authorities and now the Australian and the Turkish governments are debating over where the head should finally be buried, the Australians wanting to send it back to Turkey and the Turks wanting the Australians to take responsibility and to bury it in Bendigo with a large memorial. After all, it hasn't exactly come with papers. It could be anybody's head.

We Are Standing at the Low Stone Wall ...

We are standing at the low stone wall of a churchyard, in a village high on a ridge overlooking the border. The church is at the edge of the village and the view from the wall is panoramic, although that word does not seem to fit the time of day – near dusk, the darkness approaching – or the chill in the breeze coming in up the valley from the sea. Nor the stories that my friend is telling me, of the partisans who used to hide on the ridges opposite, the German killings, the reprisals, the raids that have lately been happening so much more. Over the border they are probably saying similar things about the people on this side, and on the far side of that country, on each side of another border, there are things being said that are almost the same. In this light the ridges look like great whales surfacing, in an already-mountainous sea.

THE WALL

It is Moon Sector 17 of what has already come to be called the Great Wall. Seven men to cover a two thousand metre stretch from the Quarter Moon guard house, westward eleven hundred metres to the gorge of the Eel River – down there, a hundred metres or so upstream, is another contingent of men, three or four, to watch for any who want to invade by water – and eastward almost nine hundred to where guards can wave at the guards of Sector 16, on the other side of the (guarded) staircase. In all weathers. Seven days a week with a half-day off each fortnight, during which the men are free to go down to the local villages – in fact to go anywhere they like – though most of them don't want to, since it's Imperial policy to send troops into provinces far away from their own, amongst unlike people, to reduce the risk of desertion. Though not, of course, of suicide, which has been known to happen. In all weather, but most often in winter, when the days are so short and so cold that seven-tenths of a guard's life is lived in the dark, or half-dark.

There is little for the guards to do but walk up and down the battlements, looking out every seven or eight metres when they come to a break just wide enough for one man to lean into and look out at more or less the same thing he looked at before, and think about jumping. Sometimes alone, sometimes in pairs (yes, the jumping, too). In the winter it's most likely to be alone, since no-one wants to leave the guardhouse, which though not exactly warm is still a great deal warmer than the outside, and has the fire, food and drink. They can't drink outside, not on duty, though in Moon Sector 17, as probably in most other sectors, no-one cares about that.

In all weathers, seven days a week. Nothing happening. Nothing ever changing, except the day of the week, the weather. No enemies visible. No-one remembering when any were. The thought coming to everyone at some time or another that the Wall was not built to keep anyone out – how could it in any case with so many gaps in it? – but to convince those on the inside that they had enemies in the first place. After all, if there is a wall, there must be something that it divides. And if it is a Great Wall then there must be a very substantial reason.

Here and there a hut is visible, a shepherd's hut, or a farmer's. And here and there a bit of track. Sometimes someone walking along it. Here and there a little human contact. Hardly a day, in fact, without human contact of a sort. It might be a wave, a shout, though most of the time the shout can't be heard properly anyway. Unless the wind is right. Walls too high, and the air too damp, winter and summer. A shout could be almost anything, and they could shout almost anything back. Up to them to decide whether it's polite or not. Only one of the seven soldiers speaks any of the local language. Not much need to, since the provisions – the food, the drink, the tobacco – are all pre-arranged, logged in by the staircase guards. And sometimes a woman, who will set herself up for a day or a night in the guardhouse before moving to another sector. Seven days a week no doubt; no doubt, like the rest, in all weathers. The frost on the ramparts, or the rain making them slippery, or the heat beating up from the stones. But mostly the frost and the rain, the stones greasy with cold. Nothing to do but walk up and down, drink, sleep, talk, fuck when they can. Think. After a year or so all arguments are argued out, all stories told. With a bit of luck there's some variation in the repetition, or they weren't listening the first time, or they've forgotten, or there's a last little coin still rattling around in someone's imagination. Every now and then someone is summoned to the staircase between the sectors and told to go home. For no apparent reason. Average time on the sector four years, give or take a year. That is, as far as anyone can tell. Four or five people sitting around comparing guesses is not much to go on. Any real idea of time requires watching it, and that only happens with new arrivals. It's just that they think, Here's summer again, how many summers is it now? Three? Four?

A bleak place. Wind, rain, ice, snow, or a summer that's so hot and dusty they long for them back again; mist for the mid-seasons. Sleep, eat, drink, fuck when they can (that's a joke: what, once every month or so, with a rough woman who talks with the rest while they do it, with another guy breathing down one's neck?), patrol the wall, think, although it's hard to tell when they're thinking and when they're not. Almost everyone gets to the point where they think that the Wall is doing their thinking for them, or at least giving them the thoughts, telling them how to think them. Almost everyone has got to the point where it occurs to them that they've had it wrong, that the side they thought was the outside, towards the enemy, is really the inside and vice versa. Almost everyone's thought that they are totally forgotten, totally abandoned. Almost everyone's thought that anyone seriously intent on being an enemy would not spend much time attacking the Wall. And if an enemy did come what would the guards do? Fight? Surrender? Offer them green tea and noodles? Wait for instructions? If there is a Headquarters anywhere it's certainly not in this province or the next, or the one after that. The Wall could be taken and it might be weeks before Headquarters knew, if anyone ever took a message in the first place.

You long for the enemy, to make sense of things.

But there is no enemy. Not in living memory anyway. Though now and again someone out there not friendly to it will try to do something to the Wall itself. Paint something on it, say – though given the way it curves there are some parts the guards them-selves could never lay eyes on (and who else could the painting be intended for?) – or steal the stones. Most of the time it is stone stealers. A hundred years ago the Wall itself took all of the stones from the fields, for a thousand metres on either side, leaving nothing for the locals to build with. Now they use the wall as a quarry. Coming by night with a horse and cart, prising away at it, getting a load of stones to build their own much smaller wall somewhere, or a stall for the cow, an outhouse. And what's a guard to do? Fire an arrow down into the dark? Drop *stones* on them? Once or twice, bold as brass, some shepherd or hermit or leper has actually tried to attach their shelter to the wall itself, though it has never been anything a little bombard-ment couldn't get rid of – that, or the guards depositing a few faeces on its roof.

That is, until this. But what *is* this? Ruins of a stone hut someone tried to build decades ago. Either that, or a shelter for the original builders of the wall. But ruins, of three walls, with the fourth wall the Wall itself. All fallen in, hardly more than an outline of stones, a bare place where the door must have been. No-one ever saw anyone there, let alone planks. Yet planks there must have been. Thick ones. Very thick ones. Brought in overnight, working fast. Overnight, or maybe over a couple of nights. No-one is admitting to not having looked, not having guarded everything, for any more than two nights at the most. But suddenly there are planks, and no-one can say for certain (to themselves: they're not giving anything away to anyone else) how long they have been there. And overnight, or over a couple of nights at the most, a roof, or lean-to, made of the planks. That perhaps a stone or two, prised from the battlement, might shift, but they don't, since the angle of the lean-to's roof is so steep there's a chance they'd just bounce off and roll into the trees. And no movement, no sign of anyone coming or going.

And yet someone is, at night, obviously. Disguising their light, if they are using one, making no sound loud enough to be heard at the top. But there, somehow; working, somehow. For after the fourth night – no-one can explain it; no-one has heard anything – the lean-to is higher, the roof just that fraction further up the wall. And so it happens, and continues to happen, very gradually. At first there is a lot of talk about it and then not much at all. Just nervous watching. Tacit agreement that if there has been no message then it's as likely to be something organised or approved by the authorities as it is to be something they don't know about, and so as likely a friendly as an enemy construction, an indication, perhaps, that they'd had their sides wrong all along, that the enemy was in fact on the side they'd thought friendly and vice versa. And there has been no message. In fact, at least while any of these soldiers have been there, there has never been a message. If they requested instructions from Headquarters it would probably be months before they heard, and by then the issue would have resolved itself or gone away. And what would they hear anyway? That they'd had it all wrong and were summoned for court martial? That reinforcements were on the way (when they might have been dead for weeks!)?

And so they watch. And, when anyone has an idea, engage in cautious, measured resistance. Until they know otherwise, they should treat it as unfriendly, for their own sake if for nothing else. Then, at least, if they are wrong, they might be alive to find out.

They pour a small vat of boiling oil. Almost half of what they have, and will have to conserve for the rest of the year. But for the time being – the roof rising a little further each week, wooden sides appearing atop the old stone base – it seems a good idea. To pour the boiling oil and then shoot flaming arrows to ignite it, burn the whole thing down. But it rains. They have been so busy with the project that they haven't noticed the clouds. A few drops at first, with the first of the arrows appearing to catch, and then a steady downpour, the oil seeming to have done nothing but help waterproof the thing (that is part of the problem, what to call it: lean-to? house? tower? thing).

A mystery. An utter, incomprehensible mystery. Sure that they can solve it, convinced that there must be some explanation, guards on night duty – especially when the moon affords some visibility – spend all night in the shadow of the battlement, watching, listening. And as first light replaces the extinguished moon find the house/lean-to/tower taller, if only by inches. What has happened? Have they fallen asleep? Have their minds wandered? Perhaps the intensity of watching can create its own illusions. When you watch something long enough it can seem to be moving, whether it's moving or not.

And then it stops, indisputably, beyond the shadow of doubt. No growth for a few weeks, even months. They watch, forget to watch, remember, watch, each in their own rhythm. Talk about it when they remember, compare notes. Someone thinks that it has grown again and gets the others to look. Sometimes they agree, sometimes not. At other times the growth is clear. How long has it been going on now? A year? A year and a half? And still no message to explain it, still nothing from Headquarters.

Indeed it seems, when they think about it, that nothing has ever arrived from Headquarters except orders for replacement followed by the replacements themselves, but the replacements themselves always come from different places and there is no reason to think that someone's replacement is heralded by anything other than a message, from further down the Wall, that a replacement is on the way. If arrival from Headquarters is the only evidence that Headquarters exists, then there is no real reason to think that Headquarters exists at all, other than that people speak about it, presume that it does.

This thing, on the other hand, while far less plausible, is here. Its walls, though timber, look very solid, are made of a hardwood that resists the sharpest arrows. Sometimes an arrow sticks for a while, if they're lucky, but only for a while, always blows off in the wind. No windows; nothing to get an arrow through; and it is built – if it can be said that something is being built when there is no evidence of builders – at such a point on the Wall that no-one can see whether there is a door at the front through which the invisible builders might come, though of course there has to be. And no-one coming or going. At one point the sergeant sits bolt upright in his bed in the middle of the night and shouts out an idea, a realisation: the tower/house/ lean-to is being built from the inside. Someone far below them has tunnelled along through the foundations of the Wall itself. The door is on the inside, not the outside. They are being undermined. For a while the Wall feels different. It is one thing to watch and wait while something encroaches from a place they can keep watch over, even if they never see anything, but an encroachment from below, within, under the very thing they're standing on, is something different again.

They renew their efforts, work on a number of plans. Lowering someone down, while the most logical thing to do, has never really been an option, since rope of any appropriate length or thickness is forbidden for fear of escape attempts. Soldiers can be allowed off the Wall one by one as their entitled half-day leave comes due, but a rope might allow all of them off at once, precipitate a group desertion. Now that the house/tower/lean-to is almost two-thirds of the way up the Wall, however, sheets and pieces of clothing might be tied together, a man might be lowered. They draw lots, send down the victor. No outside door as far as he can tell, but it is hard to see. Certainly no path anywhere, no building rubble. And the roof-planks themselves – better to call them beams – are too thick, can't be budged, even with something to prise at them. Perhaps, if he could hammer thick nails into the lower part of the lean-to roof, give himself something to stand on, make a platform, then he could hack, saw, chip his way in, but where to get the nails, the planks for a platform? Requisition them? Explain? They have left it too long, in all their indecisiveness. Now, surely, all they would get would be court martial for incompetence. Better to try to handle it themselves, since that's the way they have started. Instead of hacking their way in they could go back to burning. This time the soldier – another soldier, since they are taking turns – could set a fire, but how to do so on the steep slope of the roof?

There is a replacement. The departee is sworn to say nothing. The newcomer – always good to have a fresh mind – comes up with another idea. Wax burns, fiercely, if the heat that starts it is strong enough, and they have a good supply of candles. And it is nearly summer, and the long dry period. Let the sun dry out the wood until it is at its most burnable and then lower a man again, fix balls of wax to the sides – not the roof; fire is wasted on the roof – and light them with burning arrows or a hand-held brand. That way the flames will move upwards along the wood, have a better chance of purchase. But the man sent down, after the months of waiting, sets only himself alight, is barely brought up before the sheets burn through, spends a week moaning in the guardhouse, keeping everyone awake, before they can get him taken away.

The top of the tower/lean-to/house roof is now near the edge of the battlement. They can lean their arms in their usual place and study the grain of the wood. They can roll pebbles down its roof. They can scramble out on it with only the one sheet to hold them, and hammer on its sides. At last, surely, they should be able to see how it has been built, how it has climbed, at last they should be able to hear the builders. But nothing. Even when, not on watch, they stay up all night just to listen. The usual problems with the first morning light. The usual doubts about sleep, dreaming. At one point one of the soldiers thinks he hears a baby cry – the least plausible thing, and sure guarantee that he had been dreaming, that his mind wandered away. Another hears a faint knocking, as if someone were trying to get out, though it might have been a sound coming from much farther away.

Inch by inch, inexorably, ineluctably, inevitably, it passes the lip of the observation ledge, begins to fill in the space between two of the battlements, then – what, a month later? two? – clears the top. Not wood like the rest of it, but stone on this side, just like the stone of the Wall itself, as if this new wall were a kind of counter-Wall, if only for ten feet of it. Until something else appears, a lintel, and below it the beginnings of a thick shutter, or door. Door. Of wood that might be drilled through, though so thick, when they try, and so hard, that everything that they have breaks or falls short. How long is it now, three, four years? And a month more before the door itself, or rather doors, for they are double-opening, rise clear. Locked, it seems, from the inside; or barred, since there is no key-hole, no sign that they are intended to be opened from without. No hinges visible. But what else can they be but doors? And what else can doors that can only be opened from within be for but to let people out?

They hammer – at first relentlessly, then every time they think of it, walking past – but receive no answer. They try to employ a battering-ram, but can use only one of the benches from inside the guardhouse and by now, although the lean-to/tower/house seems to be growing no further, the doors are too high for easy reach and they have to erect a platform along which to run with the ram, so that, given the narrowness of the top of the Wall in the first place, the battering is no more use than pounding with the fist. For a time, trepidatiously, having done all this, they do nothing but wait, watch, and, when circumstances allow, sit or lean before the doors, by day or at night, listening. There is a tiny space between the bottom of the doors and the stone threshold, scarcely enough to pass a sheet of parchment, let alone shine a light through. By day, as far as can be told, there is only darkness within, although by night those who have spent a long time watching swear that a glimmer, a thin line of light can sometimes be seen, always as if at the edge of the eye, gone by the time they look back at it. Two of those who have seen it claim also, although with less confidence, that they have heard the shuffling of feet.

All of them feel a mounting nervousness. On a bleak winter day when the duty guard reports hearing a louder-than-usual sound from within, like the shifting of furniture or movement of a piece of timber, they determine, around the brazier, that they can no longer leave things as they have been, and that, if they cannot get into the house/lean-to/tower structure – 'structure', yes, that is what they should call it – they should at least ensure as best they can that who- or whatever is within it cannot get out.

Outward-opening doors without handles are hard things to bar. Wheedling the staircase guards, claiming to be fixing a large shutter that has blown off its old hinges and onto the enemy side in a high wind, they are able to get several thick planks and the materials to fasten them across the doors, using the remaining planks and one of the heavy guardhouse benches, dismantled, to create a further reinforcement, which they anchor in the battlement itself by a judicious removal of stones. Should there be forces within the structure strong enough to break through such a barrier they will at least issue some kind of warning in their attempt to do so. Such, in any case, is the theory.

There has been no growth of the structure for several months, as if the intention all along has been to reach the level at which the door is exposed and to reach that level only. A further replacement is made, this time of the sergeant himself. In the short time they have in which to discuss the matter before he has to leave he advises them to say nothing to the man who replaces him. The structure, for all that any of them knows, has been there since the construction of the Wall itself, as has the barricade to its doors. If the new sergeant wants to remove it, the departing sergeant says, or to try to do anything about the doors themselves, let him do what he can. This, he says, is their chance to absolve themselves of any responsibility. They have only to act as if the lean-to/tower/house has always been a part of the landscape, and refer any question about it to Headquarters.

The new sergeant arrives, a slight, rather sullen man from one of the southernmost provinces. Since it is the only thing, other than the guardhouse itself, to break the long, clean line of the Wall, the construction is one of the first things he asks about. The soldiers answer as they have been instructed. He is most curious but, not being one to question authority or to take any initiative when there is no apparent need for it to be taken, and presuming nonetheless that the doors would not be barred without good reason, he writes to Headquarters – that is, he presumes, or is led to presume, that the staircase guards will forward the document to someone who will forward it to someone who will forward it to Headquarters – detailing the situation as he understands it and requesting instructions.

No reply is ever received – at least, not while there is anyone still there to remember what the questions might have been in the first place. The personnel changes according to what is presumed to be the established pattern. Now and again, as if in obedience to a ritual nothing but Time itself could ever recognise, a new sergeant orders the barricade removed and the men, sweating, swearing, jarring their hands, prise it off with whatever implements they have or can find some excuse to borrow from the gatehouse. And then, finding the doors will not open outwards or in, look for a battering-ram, only to find that, the doors being too hard for easy reach, etc., given the narrowness of the top of the wall, etc. So that even Time, had it any consciousness at all, might find it hard to determine the ultimate point or fulcrum of the Event: the Wall, the Lean-to/Tower/House itself, the Barricade, the Doors, the Tapping that is sometimes heard from within, that might be human, yes, or ghostly, but is probably no more than a loose board somewhere, or shutter, far below, banging in the wind.

THE SEVENTH FLOOR

He hadn't been there the second time either, the poet. They'd come earlier, at nine-thirty, on their way back from dinner at the restaurant across the road. She'd felt like a cigarette outside – it was a non-smoking hotel – and he'd gone to check the bar, had walked through the cluster of low tables and armchairs, the poet clearly not there, then onto the terrace, and from there had looked across to where she stood by the main entrance, smoking and thinking and staring out onto the night – a moment of quiet grace and secret pleasure for him, to step away and see her from this slight distance. Within a few minutes she had turned, seen him watching, and smiled, and he had clambered through a gap in the railing, pushed through the shrubbery and walked over. No, the poet wasn't there, but he hadn't been sure, anyway – it had been so noisy at the reception – whether he'd said nine or ten, or in fact specified any time at all. Let's go back to the room, have a glass of wine on the balcony, and come back down in half an hour if we still feel like it. The poet is gregarious, he reminded her, you know him; he's probably got into some rambling conversation over dinner and forgotten the arrangement entirely.

So they had – gone up to the room, had a glass of wine on the balcony, come back down at ten, found nobody there, and gone back to the lift to go up to the room again. And beside the lift, having already pressed the button, waiting, was a woman, smiling at them warmly as they approached, holding the lift door open for them as they entered – smiling so warmly, indeed, that he wondered if she were someone who knew them, someone he should perhaps recognise, but no, he'd decided quickly, it was just friendliness. A pleasant woman, in her mid- or late-forties, ten years older than his wife, perhaps, and ten or so younger than him. Attractive, with a nice mouth, an aura of summer grass. And something had happened between the ground and the seventh floor. An intimate gesture, it must have been. Not that he had seen it, just known, somehow, that it had occurred. Not even voluntary, most likely, perhaps not even something one could be conscious of. And there had been no time to think, no time to stop what he'd found himself doing, to question the propriety of it, the sanity. A dilemma. He'd had no right to speak and no right not to. Sometimes a thought comes to mind and there is nothing else one can do but to act upon it.

'Excuse me!' he'd said, as she'd left – leaning out of the lift, holding the door open himself now. 'We've just decided to go back down, for a nightcap. Would you like to join us?' And, just as spontaneously – as if the gesture, if that is what it had been (but whose *had* it been?) had already made sense of things, even before the idea had arrived – she had accepted.

They had ordered a bottle, a famous, elegant white wine from the Cape – he was quietly celebrating, he'd explained, telling her of the award he was about to receive – and then, after just the one glass, he'd excused himself, said that he was feeling more tired than he thought and needed his rest, and, leaving them there, insisting that they stay, had gone up again to the eleventh floor.

It hadn't taken him long to go to sleep. The double-glazed windows opened in the European way, inward from the top, and there had been a breeze, cooling and soporific after the heat of the day, so that he'd not pulled the heavy drapes, but let instead the thinner, transparent curtains catch the soft light of the moon and the distant streetlamps. He had gone over the lines of an old song – he could never tell when it would come back to him – again and again, trying to get them right. Somewhere between the third and the fifth verses, at a point he'd stumbled upon, over and over, for so much of his life now, he fell asleep, and couldn't have said how much later it was – but there was no sound of traffic, and the room had a long-after-midnight cool – that he half-woke to see her undressing with the billowing curtain about her, then felt her climb in, naked, and put her arm around him.

In the morning, as they'd showered and dressed, they'd said nothing. There was no need. Halfway down on their way to a late breakfast, however, with no-one else in the lift, she'd suddenly turned and kissed him, that was all, lightly and gently on the lips, and he'd asked, at last, how it was. 'Nice,' she'd said. 'It was nice,' smiling softly. 'She had a nice mouth.'

GRIEF

We are early – have to be, to greet the mourners – and sitting on a bench beside the open coffin. A strict ritual. Knowledge passed from funeral to funeral, by those who have been to so many. There has been discussion as to whether her face should be lightly veiled, as it was when we entered and the lid was first removed, or uncovered. Aldo wants it uncovered, and it's at last his say. His mother. For some reason the funeral directors have made no attempt to disguise the wounds on her face and I can see now how large they are. But they are on her right side and we are seated on her left. Aldo touches her cheek tenderly – brushes it, rather, with the edge of his hand – then leans over, kisses her on the forehead. It is the first time I have ever seen him kiss her.

~

I am still thinking about the cat. A lingering image on the mind's retina. A dying glow. You look into the light – at some lit object – and then close your eyes, and the light, the shape of the object is still there, blurred at the edges, its features lost; some force emanating from within. Except that in this case it was not light. Was, and was not. Is not. A tunnel vision. A vortex down which, since it happened, I am always falling yet never seeming nearer or farther away. A kind of vertigo. And the mountains today like great waves there on the horizon, about to engulf us.

~

The old lady died on the Tuesday. Sad, but no great surprise. I'd heard her from the rooms below, for six weeks or more, shouting, calling out names, lost in the corridors of herself. Long days of silence and then it would break out again. She would. I don't know what brought it on. The wind maybe. Or some weather inside her. Katia told me of her death almost matter-of-factly as I was talking with Igor on the balcony. There'd been a phone call in her study, and she came out. 'Nona just died,' she said, 'at the hospital a few minutes ago. That was my father. He's there.' And we went on with our day, tentatively, not knowing what else to do, waiting for something to arrive, to break.

~

A nausea, perhaps. The overwhelming weight of being. But also something more, surely. The heart was *wrenched*, as if something had prised it open. The opposite of nausea. Not closed in by things, but *offered* them, in their depth. Or drawn *by* them, *rushed into* them. As if one were being sucked out of oneself. A force. A kind of gravity. The cat at its centre, there in the boot-room.

~

At Alex's, while we talked at the table inside, our chairs angled towards the French doors so that we could see the view, the cats came, four, with a fifth somewhere off in the forest – dying,

Jacqueline said. All of them were scrawny, under-nourished. Jacqueline fed them but they never fattened. Village cats. Worm-ridden probably. Katia always annoyed that Alex and Jacqueline didn't pay them more attention, offer more affection, *see* their condition. Katia rescued a white kitten two years ago, bonded with her instantly on the lawn, took her home. In twenty-four months she's become sleek, independent, strong. Bianca. At the window, late at night, while I read. Waiting for entrance. 'That one's Bianca's mother,' Jacqueline says, pointing out a gaunt, long-haired tabby, oldest of the four. Looking as if she might be dying too. 'No,' says Jacqueline, reading our minds, 'She has always looked like that.' So many cats in these villages. You'd think *they* were the inhabitants, not humans.

~

This late afternoon – this late afternoon and on into the evening – I have watched a mass of clouds gather in the north-east and darken to a deep bruise-purple, and felt the pressure mounting within them, electrical, torrential. Couldn't it be like that? The Outside? And now, just moments ago, the first light-ning. A crack. A fissure in the sky.

~

Igor left, in any case, not knowing what to do. I waited for Aldo to return from the hospital, anticipating his grief. But when he came back he put the car away, went into the down-stairs kitchen for a while, then came out and went down to the fields. Perhaps he was sobbing down there. I don't know. And as to what Katia was feeling, there are times I can't tell that either, especially when it comes to family. Her grandmother hated cats. And Katia had claimed to hate her grandmother for hating them.

~

You carry such things around with you. I was sitting on the terrace of that strange hotel a hundred kilometres away, a fortnight later. Who ever heard of a hotel room without a table, a chair? And so I'd come downstairs. It was quiet on the terrace, and shaded by the building, out of the sun. A broad, calm view of slopes covered with trellised vines, mountains capped with snow even at this late stage of summer. And in the vineyard just below the terrace a dirt track, leading off along the edge of the vines, turning at the end into a small wooded area, disappearing from sight. What is it about a track that makes one walk along it in one's mind, wonder what one would see? Grasshoppers, I thought suddenly, or a butterfly, a large bee on some thick clover beneath a vine-stock. And silence. There would be silence. That as soon as you listened to it would be full of busyness, the constant whispering and shuffling of things, the breathing that becomes almost a hum, a soft shrillness answering from within. Would the track reach the mountains, if I followed it? This dream, of all tracks merging, everything connecting, drawing you …

~

As the priest delivered the eulogy I was looking at the stones. The cracks in them, the spaces between, the broken places. Filled with crumbled mortar. Here and there droppings that Danaja's broom didn't catch. Of mice, not rats. Too small for rats. Evicted temporarily but watching from somewhere. Rafters, cracks in the walls. To come out and re-occupy when all was finished. This chapel not much used. Another year, two, before the next disturbance. Light filtering through dust motes. Tiredness in the priest's voice, or just a studied calm, as he went through the formulae, holding something at bay. That hugeness inside us, outside us.

~

She had fallen. I had been working at my desk and there'd been a commotion below, muted: I couldn't hear any sign of panic. A dragging of furniture, metal frame on tile, that can only have been her bed. Without the language I can't help much, think I am only in the way. And others were there in any case. And then, ten minutes later, Aldo, asking for Katia though he knew she wasn't here. And explained, although I only half-understood. Except that he needed to tell. I understood that. That she had fallen. Hurt herself. And went away, with a kind of shrug. His shrug. As much to the world as to me.

A few minutes later an ambulance arrived. I watched from the upstairs window as they brought her out. She looked unconscious, head back as if in mid-gasp, a wound on her cheek, another above her eye. Not much blood. Why do I think it thickens, in the elderly, almost reluctant to leave?

~

He had been there, Aldo, in the hospital, at her bedside. She'd complained of feeling sick, wanting to vomit, and he'd called for a nurse. By the time someone came she'd passed out and her eyes had rolled back. They had taken her away, and left him there waiting. Soon they returned and told him she had died.

He told this to Katia that night, late, after I had gone to bed. They would not use the church for the funeral, nor the priest, not this one. No surprises there. They'd use the small chapel in the cemetery instead, and arrange for someone else to come. They'd have to spend the next day cleaning. The chapel stank of mice – or rats, who knew? Katia thought rats – and there were droppings everywhere. I offered to help, but no, she'd do it with Danaja. It was all arranged.

~

I don't remember when it was I saw the moth. On the light-fitting over the sink. There are moths here day and night during the summer, as there are anywhere when you leave the doors and windows open to catch the night air. Souls, people say. Psyche. This one of a bright green I've never seen on a moth before. Uniform, unvariegated, the colour of a grass-blade in late-summer sun. An after-image of day. But why? So that I would see it? Carry it into my sleep? As if it needed a ride somewhere, and I were a psychopomp.

~

Katia is at loggerheads with the priest, a new appointee. Over an old transgression, on his part not hers. When they were at university together. A drunkard, and violent. She's had him banned from the house, by order of the bishop who's been inundated with calls to bring back the previous priest. His response to ban the previous priest from the parish entirely so that the new one can get on with it. But now Nona is dead, and Katia's parents have bitten the bullet, gone to the bishop's house, caught him and his minions at breakfast. He'd have looked petty to refuse. A special dispensation. The previous priest allowed back, just this once.

~

Heavy rain the night before the funeral. Air clear in the morning, all the haze washed out. The far mountains outlined clear against the sky, mist like a white skin on the plain, peaks floating above it unanchored, cut adrift. I'd been worried that the grave had already been dug and would now be filled with water, but no, they must watch the weather. Came early in the morning and dug it then. Three men, who by the time the funeral had commenced had changed into suits. In the same small plot as her husband, dead forty-five years now. How would they do it? Dig until they find a trace of him and then place her on top? His coffin rotted now, surely. Gone. These things you don't think about until you need to. So many bodies in that small cemetery. And how will they manage with me? Not so hard I suppose. I will be ashes in a jar. Katia will hold me.

~

A thought crosses the mind. Or is it a vision, a glimpse? This of the moth – *as if I were with it* – in the garden somewhere, feather-light in the corners of darkness. Dreaming me, moving on.

~

A week after. The eighth-night Mass. Has she been waiting, for this final permission? Aldo is anxious that he not have to go alone, but the church is being painted; the first floor of the gallery next door is to be used instead. And Lucia, Katia's mother, is still on crutches after her operation, can't handle the stairs. He comes to ask Katia to go with him, knowing full well her fury with the church, and she too at first refuses – he has left it too late, the dinner is already on the table – but then unexpectedly relents. Leaves the meal half-eaten. She will be half an hour, no more.

I sit and watch the sunset. Half an hour, forty-five minutes, an hour. People are walking back from the Mass in first darkness. More people than I would have thought, but then Nona has been here a very long time. And then suddenly, from the courtyard, Katia's voice calling, urgent. I go to the landing. She is holding something to her chest. A cat, she says, and it's dying, might be dead already, she can't tell. Bring water. Bring food. By the time I get down she has laid it on its right side on the floor of the boot-room. She rushes into the house to get a syringe, so that she can feed it water drop by drop.

I watch it in the pool of yellow light, can see no movement. Long, thick hair, matted, gaunt, either very old or very ill. Both. It must weigh almost nothing but already the gravity has flattened it against the tiles. It. Him. Her. Such sad stillness. And then suddenly the right forepaw stretches, lunges almost, a spasm, and goes limp again. Within seconds Katia is back and tries to coax it to drink from the syringe, but the water simply runs out onto the floor. We place rags in the alcove at the side and she moves it there. There is no resistance in its body. It droops in her hands like something already far off. As we finish our dinner she tells me the story. That she'd seen the cat in the grass by the road as she was walking to the Mass, sick, obviously dying, and straight afterward had run back there, to find that it had moved to the other side. Robbie had called from his porch to say that it had been there for three days already, and the woman next door to him had been feeding it. She had checked next door; no-one was there; so she had gathered it up and brought it home. When

I express consternation that people have been walking past it for days and that no-one has taken it to a vet, she tells me that I still don't know these people. For them it's just a cat. *It*, not *he*, not *she*.

~

It was later, just after ten, I think. I had been reading some dry philosophy, bored, skimming, looking for something. I suppose you could say my mind wandered, without in any way signalling that it was doing so. And there was a sudden tunnel, a *vision*. I was looking at the cat – although it was impossible, although I was at my desk and it was downstairs and across the courtyard, in the boot-room – as if through a portal, or port-*hole*, surrounded by darkness, in a pool of hot, rancid light. And had just realised what I was seeing – that it *was* the cat, so deep and so burdened with its dying – when the wave struck and whelmed over me and I was submerged in it, fighting for breath. Of anguish, a sadness beyond measure. And I was standing there, before Katia, there was nowhere else to go, the sobs breaking from me, despite all I could do to hold them.

When I slept at last it was to dream of a body discovered, a century after a shipwreck, frozen in Antarctic ice, and then of a bubble rising with unbearable slowness through a tar-like substance – a bubble that had been rising for millennia – at last reaching the surface, releasing its ancient, rotten air.

~

The mourners are filing by, grasping our hands as they pass. Condolences. With twenty minutes still to go before the priest arrives most of them are seated, in silence, thinking, waiting.

A very pious man in a back row – Katia has pointed him out as the bishop's informer – takes out his beads and begins to say the rosary, and suddenly, as if a wave has swept over the room, the whole congregation of elderly women, elderly men, has joined him. Breaking from dry throats, scarcely more than a rasping at first, wind through dry grass, the prayer builds, pushing its way through voices almost too tired to stand, finding its passages, a bass drone slowly filling the space as water fills a jug. Groaning up through the stones, an ancient poetry underneath, within, of grief and bewilderment, incomprehension, overlaid by the old rituals and recipes of containment, this chanting of the rosary, people burying their own dead again, any funeral a reawakening, reburying, re-grieving, mothers, fathers, daughters, brothers, friends, wives, husbands, again, in slow showers of earth, insubstantial, heavy as this shadow, out of the afternoon sunlight, her death mask almost beautiful in its rest, after the torment, waxen, pearl-grey, the fright and confusion become dignity, music moving through us in a kind of praise, making us instruments, wind, clay vessels, a kind of brooding bird, almost dove.

LOST PAGES

It's a constant temptation of the human to invest the unknown with ulterior meaning, to see in the gaps of its own understanding some purposeful hand beyond. But how else explain the lost pages? The lines, the whole tracts of thought gone. If I can't get them back it's surely time they had some epitaph, though even in proposing such a thing there's trepidation, apprehension that this, too, will mysteriously evaporate before it sees the light of day. Although perhaps it could be seen as some kind of test: proof positive, if this also goes missing, and proof negative if it does not, although such might also be a nefarious attempt to obscure the matter.

~

It was a familiar joke, a story to be told while drinking or after dinner at Sarafini's, a whimsy to most of his writer friends, although to him in solitary moments – moments of self-doubt or envy – also a matter of regret, resentment, even mourning. The Night of the Lost Pages. The Night of the Grand Illumination. It had been his own fault, perhaps, for telling the story with such self-irony, for making so light of it. As they all did: it was their manner. As if Truth had been ruled out finally and after all. There had been a divergence, at the tip of his tongue, a fork, and he had taken the wrong path. But since he had first told the story it had served as a magnet for other tales like it. M, for example, reminding him of the draft of the poem that he, M, had left on a seat on a suburban train, or J telling him of A's notebooks, twenty years of ideas and reflections lost in an office fire. One by one almost all of the group had added some tale of their own, or brought him a story from a book they had been reading, a conversation they had just had: of the first draft of V's novel left in a book-shop where he had been browsing and never seen again, of H's wife burning what she thought to be his outrageous confessions, of S's husband feeding her diaries to the fire on the twentieth anniversary of her death.

If everything that we write, every word-thing we create, is carved out of silence, chaos, emptiness, the vast Outside, it stands to reason, doesn't it, that the winds or currents of that chaos, that silence outside us, will sometimes make off with a portion of it, and

*will carry it far beyond reach. But if it stands
to reason, that may be all that it stands to,
and doesn't account for the nagging pattern
of such depredations, the way so many of
them seem to bear upon the same channels
of thought, seem to hover about the same
subjects, the same borders.*

~

Although, in the works of Heinborn, there is
nothing specifically on textual loss, Gilberto
Raimondi, the most perceptive of his biog-
raphers, argues that such was not only a
logical extension of his work, but an actual
subject, though a subject that itself, as if in
demonstration of Heinborn's own theories
of Omission ('The Aetiology of Omission',
1933), did not survive the destruction of his
papers. But by the same token, since there is
no omission that does not leave its *residue*, this
possible subject can, from hints, fragments,
implications – those verbal *raised eyebrows*
for which Heinborn is so famous – be recon-
structed. In one of the notorious 'secret
seminars' in the unofficial conference on his
work at Clermont-l'Hérault in 1955 he is said
to have spent the first hour speaking of *that
of which he was not able to speak*, given that,
on the train from Düsseldorf, he had 'lost'
the first section of his lecture, a trope which
some immediately suspected to have been

an invention in demonstration of the very *Verschwinden* (disappearance) that was his subject.

~

The Night of the Lost Pages. In fact, when he first thought of it like that, no pages *per se* had been lost at all, only the script that should have been on them. He had woken in the pitch dark with a thought in his mind that he had not wanted to lose – something that had come from a dream – and so had got up and found his notebook and a pen, and written it down. As he was about to return to bed, a last, precautionary codicil had struck him – one idea so often led to another – and he had picked up the writing materials and, turning off the light in the study, walked back through the dark house to the bedroom. Crossing the foyer he had dropped the ballpoint pen but, having heard where it clattered on the tiles, had been able to find it without turning on the light and had continued to the bedroom. Ten minutes later, in bed, on cue, as if the initial thought – it had been little more than an image – had been only an advance guard, a warning, an entire argument had come to him, an answer to a metaphysical problem that had been troubling him for years. And so simply, so clearly could he see it now, that it might have been an exact formula, a philosophical principle as clear as that of Pascal's Wager, or at the very least one of the aphorisms of Schopenhauer.

Afraid that if he went back to the study he would lose it, so brightly and urgently did it appear, and yet not wanting to wake Grace by turning on the reading-light – knowing, too, how light can dissipate the focus – he had sat on the edge of the bed in the dark writing it all out in note-form over four or five pages, the words burning, glowing within him, a trace, a gem, a gift such as comes to even the greatest writers only a handful of times in their career. And then had lain there, heart racing, the ramifications spread out before him like a grand vista, a wide landscape of thought, and eventually slept profoundly, as if the thinking itself – the receiving – had exhausted him.

The next morning, remembering, he had turned immediately, excitedly, to see what he had written, only to find that the ballpoint had been damaged by its fall, and that, apart from an occasional sputtering, there was almost no trace of the lucid, inspired writing he had done, and of which now, so deeply had he slept, he remembered little more than the exuberance and an occasional haunting word or phrase.

A morning of intense frustration followed as he tried by all means he could think of to rescue the text. But the most careful, most delicate rubbings only served to increase his disappointment as he found the pressure applied – the scoring of the inkless pen – to one side of the page had been rendered only the more illegible by the pressure applied by the pen to the obverse. Where he could

produce any image at all it resembled not text so
much as a writing of snakes.

~

as late this afternoon, when,
after a storm, with another storm
promising - the day having been
hot though overcast, as humid as
a sauna - he set out for the beach
and a swim in the grey swell. He
had hardly reached the top of Carr
Street when the first idea came to
him, of something - a story? an
essay? - about the Language of Birds.
Not the one/s they speak themselves,
but how the names we have for them
are so inadequate, so misleading,
signifiers floating above the signified.
All the birds missed or not caught
in its net. All the 'stages' of
birds that don't fit into the simple
descriptions of 'immature' or 'adult'
that the field guides provide. All
the colour-forms between one 'stage'
and another. All the exotic, blown
or travelling birds that are not
supposed to be where we see them.
The idea getting no further than this
before the next idea crossed it like
static from a new place and he had
begun, only a block further down the

107

three-block hill, to think more of
the birds in *this* place, or, rather,
this place that the birds were in.

~

B. suggests that this *is* mere paranoia, that it is
only a matter of brain cells dying, but how could
that contribute? We use only a small portion of
the brain's capacity. Who is to calculate the effect
of a minuscule attrition of what is already only
partly employed?

~

Dead text. Lost text. Text that has broken
itself against the impossible. **Boulder**
Or been broken, cracked from within.
Shattered by something it couldn't
contain. Was too fragile. Iron text,
rusted. Corroded by time. Acid in the
air. The rain. You see them. Beached in
the grass. At the Aral Sea. Those boats.
Or on the edges of the Danube. Near
Linz. Near Galati. Words painted on
their bows. Barely legible. Some dream.
Some intention. *in the* Footprints. Idea
gone off. Beyond finding. The tracker not
capable. You *see* but there is not the will.
Not passage. Words locked in silence.
Pages like arctic ice. And the sewers. The
threaders. Of fragments. These ragged

clothes. The sewers. A murrain. Terminal. Breccia. **heart's** 'Nothing / left but a / mind / flaring'. 'As if'.

~

But in truth it was hardly the first time. Never before such a revelation, perhaps – never before a thought of such brilliance, such clarity, resolving so much (but that was all he remembered, the feeling that it would resolve, that it had, just then, *resolved*) – but small, glowing fragments of a puzzle one might at some point piece together, or *seeds*, that with careful nurturing might grow into a poem, say, or story. On a filing card, a bus ticket, a docket from the supermarket, fallen from one's pocket as one fumbled for change, or accidentally discarded in some pile of now irretrievable wastepaper, or slipped somewhere into the leaves of a book in one's impossible library – lost, or if, as sometimes happened, found again – for sometimes they *were* found – found also to have been sketched with ridiculous, self-defeating self-confidence, with too many lacunae, too many passages marked by dots, to be filled out later with things now far beyond the mind's recall. Forgotten, if it was an idea before the idea before sleep, in the absurd belief that it would somehow be remembered in the morning. So that it was not a page, a phrase, a word that was lost, so much as a connection within, and only oneself to blame.

Perhaps, he thought, trying to explain this, it was the loss itself – its power to fixate one – that gave these thoughts their apparent value, the way one can become almost obsessed over a lost glove, a spanner, when one could so easily go out and buy others. But mightn't it be, too, that it was something in the thoughts themselves that could not allow them to be uttered? The sudden, awe-ful thought – ridiculous, yes, paranoid, yes, but none-theless awful for that – that there was Something, Someone, against all his scepticism, all his disbe-lief, and that that Thing, that Being could not allow what he had uttered – what he had *thought* to utter – to be written, to be published, to be seen. A Thing? A Being? Or was it a system, *the* System, so deep, so filamentous that it operated through him or around him, in the night, in the patterns of waste, in the patterns of luck, so as to cancel out a part of him, so as to have *him* cancel a part of himself? (For might it not, also, be he himself, some part of *him*, who was not allowing, as the writing came close to something – some secret, from the dark field of secrets – so deeply hidden, so repressed, that when a fragment surfaced, or some fragment upon the surface resonated, some other part, some guardian of the subconscious snatched that fragment from sight …)

~

… as if in an age … *I once typed, rapidly into a file on my word processor in that tiny*

room on rue Buci, when we have done away
with such lordly imperatives, there are
words which <u>may not be spoken</u>, thoughts
which <u>may not be thought</u>, or the doing
away with imperatives were itself a veiled
imperative ... *And then, most bizarre of all,
looked up at what I had just keyed, to find
that, as had never happened before, what I
had written had leapt into large letters – had
I entered a command I did not know
about? – shouting at me, as if a part of* me
were shouting at myself, *trying to warn me:*
words which <u>may not be spoken</u>,
thoughts which <u>may not be
thought</u>

~

... kite. And she had thought it was
the thing of paper I was speaking of
but I meant of course the raptor, and
the shadow of the wing, touching
the mind, something as fleeting, as
evanescent as that, as it swooped, on
its own business ...

*

She tells me, in another mood, that there are
some things that are simply unspeakable, and that
writing, whatever else it might be, is also a seeking-
out of these, that they are a curse *and point* of it. Why

is it, she asks me, that whenever someone writes about Yen Dokla – the sheer abject horror of what occurred there – they find themselves in the middle of legal action, accusations of plagiarism, their integrity and ability in question, unless there were not some unconscious communal agreement that this were a wordless place, a not-to-be-spoken, or the horror were somehow un-writable, a silence that art cannot break? To write strongly and powerfully the horror of things, she says, doesn't one have to resort to techniques, tropes, mouldings of sounds and words that belong to the realm and mind of art, not of the reality and the horror? To *speak* it, in this sense, *is* to betray. To make language powerful, she tells me, is also to take it away. Something else – weakness, deprivation, erosion, loss – becomes necessary if we are going to intimate or locate the unspeakable, if we are going to *say* it.

~

Night-thoughts often, from my insomnia,
when one writes in the dark, fumbling for
the pen and the book beside the bed, writing
by feel on a page one prays is blank, the
words sometimes running off the paper's
edge, hoping that in the flow of a thought
or image one has not forgotten oneself and,
failing to space the lines carefully by finger-
breadths, over-written one's own writing so
that, line laid upon line, word scrawled upon

word – the breaks between words, on one line,
obliterated, bridged over, by the words of the
over-writing line – one has created only an
indecipherable knot, a kind of black mass …

~

Reminding us of Freud's statement that there is no such thing as accident – tracing it, humorously, back through Napoleon and Schiller – Raimondi, reconstructing from hints and fragments the position of the Heinborn, a position which he describes as the *lacuna* about which all the philosopher's work turns, argues not only that those things which are lost are *deliberately* so, as modes of repression, but that the loss does not come from within the individual, as a form of psychosis, but from without, given that the individual is a *social construct*, and is best conceived as infiltrated, from the point of his/her inception, by devices – psychosocial *strategia* – that filter discourse, determine what may or may not pass utterance. You 'lose' text; you 'lose' pages; your computer 'swallows' a fragment, a paragraph, a document, a month's work, but it is never 'accident'.

~

A barricaded village hemmed in by snow, wolves and mounted

marauders, struggling to keep them at bay. True, a thought only. But who is to say that, even as these words are written, it is not being snuffed out, as the first gates are smashed, the first of the invaders break through, homes, barns, woodpiles already blazing from the burning arrows?

~

CLEAR night words – or, if not clear, at least the spidery-because-unseeing hand decipherable – leading to a furrow or trench where two other lines cross and for a short space – four or five words – write over. As if another animal had used the same narrow pass, obliterating the tracks of the first. Memory, partial as it is, suggests one thing, although attempts to decipher the scrambled lines do not seem to support it:

that   ,a   ssing
    but I
      pages   ssing
         utterable as   they
    ggling

               dismiss

  its

~

Raimondi, in *The Hidden Heinborn* (1986),
identifies the thread of a counter-movement,
a kind of rescue. Whereas Schiller, Napoleon,
claim there is no accident because all is in
fact *fate*, Heinborn demurs, although in a
manner that suggests he is himself battling
with his own in-filt(rat)ers, telling a tale of a
philosopher, on the very margins of empire,
exiled amongst savages, believing he is alone,
and that the insights to which he has at last
come, into the mind of empire, will die
with him, unaware that the weakest point of
empire, its periphery, is so not only because
it is here that it meets its as-yet-unconquered
resistance, but because it can be only so long
before those internal resisters banished to it
realise, counter-intuitively, that they are not
alone, and that, in their very isolation, they
have a power they had not thought they
had. What are the implications for what has
been lost? Is there hope of retrieval? Has he
identified – embodied – that loss, within the
person of the exiled man *who does not know
that he is not alone*?

~

Save continually, B. says, back everything up.
But even this will not stop it. There is a kind of
rent that you pay to the Machine. A word here,
an emended sentence there, a whole set of edits
and corrections, a lapse of concentration, a

mis-filing, a careless or accidental deletion. At last, she says, we've come to a point, a technology, where — *to all appearances* — words can *dis*appear without trace, or where only the True Adepts, the Technocrats, can retrieve them. There are also, out there, the viruses, that can be imported, can infiltrate, obeying some other program, cutting swathes through our documents, eating whole fields of text.

~

How there had been difficulty getting
here this time - how *they* had had
difficulty - and he had been afraid
he'd lost his connection, his link
to it, which would be like losing a
sacred centre, one of the few he had,
maybe the only, and how, perhaps, he
should write this down, all of it,
in a journal entry, or in a letter
to someone, but before he had worked
much on the idea, and by now at the
foot of Carr Street, on the top of
the beach track, he found himself
making, still only in his mind, a
different kind of journal entry, on
a further idea the previous idea had
suggested. But by the time he had
found the first words for this he was
slipping down the grassy sand-ledge to
the beach itself, and taking off his

clothes, and was soon swept up in the
enchantment and exhilaration of the
waves and the twilight and the utterly
deserted place - his only companion a
reef heron stepping slowly along the
far edge of the tidal lagoon - and
the rain which then started and
continued while he swam and body-
surfed, soaking his clothes up on the
beach and stippling the sea's surface.
His thinking, there, on the fringe
of the continent, that he had come
somehow to an edge of things, if only
of a day full of people, uncertain
weather, the frustrations of packing
while the storm threatened, the
driving through the earlier teeming
rain (the heavens had opened around
Nara), arguments ...

~

Yen Dokla. The forest. Of which no-one
in that city will speak, so few historians
even make mention. And yet, as the
regime was crumbling, I found, in a small
worker's cottage by the railway, an old
man – it was his son who had summoned
me, having heard that I had been making
enquiries – who seemed to want abso-
lution. He had never spoken, he said, for,
in the early years, he had watched the fate

of anyone who had. But a survivor – there *had* been a survivor – had told a group of them, and presumably others. And had subsequently disappeared. The regime had tracked him. Three thousand in one night, that man had said. And those who had done the shooting were themselves shot, a long way away, taken there so that those who then shot them would not know why they were doing so.

~

So THAT *now he has only to pause, in something he is reading, pause and stare, for the paragraph to begin to disintegrate, the sentences break up and drift apart, each word seeming only a fragment of a lost original, each phrase just a trace of a now-obliterated, undecipherable text beyond it ... no matter what truth, what verisimilitude the writer might be seeking to establish, sheet-ice, breaking up beneath the runner, fathomless sea beneath ...*

~

Carrying his wet clothes in a bundle as he climbed back up the hill in the near-dark, all he could think

of was a hot shower. And it was
only then, luxuriating in the hot
water, that he began to think of
the jewels again, and found them
so ordinary – but – the *un*ordinary
thing – realised at least what had
happened, and what it was just
possibly a part of, the business of
the Lost Pages, this time of the tail
of something – he thought of it,
for a moment, melodramatically, as
the great kite of Nothingness – that
had passed overhead, again, and the
realisation that (again) he had not
caught it. And so wrote/is writing,
this, as a record of that passing ...

~

And yes, it's all very well to say that
with a little careful attention one
should be able to find the end of the
narrow pass, the over-trodden track,
and take up the trace once more, but
there, at the other end, although the
two paths divided again and went on
their separate ways, there seemed – as
if in proof of the power of what I had
so carelessly obliterated – nothing to
connect them to their former selves.
What had been a doe was now a fox;
what had been a goat was now a stag;

119

what had been a wood was now a
crowd of faces.

~

*You trawl your mind for a phrase, write down
what you find, use it as bait for others. With
luck more will come and you will find yourself
with a scattering of them, each feeling out for
the others, some connecting by themselves,
others suggesting new connections to you.
Today, for example, it was the story of the
photocopier, the walk in the park, the necks
of the doves. You spread them out before you,
trying to remember the idea as it first came, the
shape that was lost in the welter of phone calls,
interruptions. You had been walking across the
Tuileries, and stopped amongst a small flock
of birds on the grass. Everything had seemed
suddenly so clear and so sensuous, as if a
needle had passed through the most disparate
things, threading them together. The doves
had invested you with their secrets. The words
as they formed in your mind had passed over
their proffered necks like fingers. And you had
sat down immediately, at the nearest bench,
to write down this sudden understanding, the
phrases polished, clear, exact. A poem it was,
a fragment of reality no less tangible than
reality itself. But then, two days later, visiting
Claude in the Bibliothèque, you had been
persuaded to copy your notes, to insure against*

loss; travelling is so dangerous, he said. And this one sheet, this one sheet only, passed into the photocopier and did not come out, neither it nor its copy, and not a thing you did could retrieve it. You had opened the machine but found nothing, and a week later the man who had come to service it – Claude had called you – invited you to look even deeper inside. Nothing, of course: nothing. And all you have now is the trace, the report, as of someone who has seen a ghost, or an angel, and knows it, and will never believe otherwise.

～

We should look not at the fragments, B. insists, but at the gaps, the spaces between. These are the cities and the highways of a dark landscape, she says, or the beginnings of them. She says that within all of us there is a kind of tiny capillary like a lane or a neglected path in a wood that connects us — that would lead us, eventually, if we could follow it, to one of these highways, one of these cities. Except that we can't follow it, at least not with language. The fragments we sometimes find ourselves with, that disappear or fall apart in our hands, are a kind of accident, a slipping of silence, into an illusion of language. It's not just lost pages, after all, she says, but lost sentences, lost phrases, lost words, lost sight, lost will.

～

one must tread/proceed so
carefully, as if between the
rocks where
emptiness

~

The heavens *did* open, and not
infrequently, and much of what
then seemed to be revealed had been
preserved. It was this that troubled
him – that he could not actually say
that the quick of things/heart of the
system *had* been withdrawn, but only,
here and there, some marginal note,
some particular formulation, some key
or trace to something that may not
have been quick or core or system
at all, and the nagging, paradoxical
suspicion this left him with, that
what hitherto had *seemed* <u>quick</u> or
<u>heart</u> or <u>core</u> *may not have been so*,
for the very reason *that it <u>had</u> so
seemed*, and that the losses of which
he was actually aware, and which it
had never before occurred to him
to piece together – which nobody
he knew had ever yet suspected or
attempted to connect – might hold
a clue to a different heart or
system entirely. The possibility,
then, that some hitherto quite

unsuspected method – some actual
cartography of loss, could that ever
be devised – might lead him to a
heart, a core, a quick he had never
yet imagined. *If It can be seen it
is not It.* And the equally nagging
suspicion that, *could* he trace
it, could he write any of it down,
perhaps the only thing he should
consider himself sure of was that he
had therefore found nothing, that he
had not traced it at all. (This, for
example – this very paragraph, which
he had risen at 3.30 a.m. to write,
trying to ensure that it not be among
those potential pages all too often
lost in failure to rise, in the
too-quick succumbing to the seduction
of sleep: would it be here when he
returned, after returning to sleep,
signifying by its very existence that
it signified nothing? He almost prayed
that it would disappear, and yet was
it not also just faintly possible
that, in order to truly mislead him,
some fragment of the truth, once
accidentally detected thus, might
be preserved, in order that it might
continue safely, *un*detected or at
least unconfirmed, in the guise of
falsehood?)

~

The cold snow. All night it snows.
Blanketing everything. The village
silent. The fires extinguished. Nothing
left to resist the whiteness that, in the
morning, covers the huts, the paths,
the bodies. Only here and there a few
sticks exposed, the frame of a burned
hut, or cart, black against the snow,
like a hieroglyph.

HORSES

'It's a bit of a maze,' she told him as they were making off under the arch at the edge of the office garden. She wasn't sure that it was, but that is what Mr Bannister had said as he'd shown her around on her first day three years earlier, and she had been saying it ever since. People would get lost, especially in their grief, and it was good to offer them an excuse. And so they wound off through the Elysian Grove, up and over the small rise, towards the Forest of Peace, one of the new allotments, to look for N4.26. Saying nothing – for what was there to say, after all? one didn't intrude – though she was looking back all the time to make sure that he was alright and that she wasn't walking too fast. He seemed a bit unsteady, with that stick.

At one point he paused. She sensed it immediately, and paused with him. On the path through the Salmon Gums, to listen to a bird. She didn't recognise the call, but clearly it meant something to him, since he looked up and about him in the branches, half-smiling, as if he'd not heard such a sound in a long time, and then, the bird stopping – he hadn't been able to see it – moved on.

And they came to it. Easy enough, even if you'd never been to that part of the cemetery before, since the N meant the North, the city side, and the 4 meant the quarter (they always worked clockwise) between nine and twelve o'clock. *John Arlington Heigh*, it read, *1940-2009, Beloved husband of … Beloved father of … The Peace That Passes All Understanding*, one of her favourite phrases.

They stood there a few moments, as if it had been a destination for her as well as him, but then, realising, snapping out of her brief daydream, she looked at him – a strange, gypsy-like man with his thick moustache and his long white hair in a straggly ponytail. Rather like Johnny Depp might look, she thought to herself, in his seventies – and his eyes turned to her, though they seemed miles away.

'I'd better be getting back,' she murmured, and asked him whether he would be alright, finding his own way. He nodded – it could have been a nod – and she left, but within twenty paces, amongst the trees at the edge of the plot, she stopped and turned. He seemed so lost. Perhaps, if he wasn't going to be too long – people were never very long – she could wait there, unobtrusively, and keep him company to the entrance when he was finished. She stepped back into the shade.

Carefully he moved over to the grave next door to John Arlington Heigh and leant his cane on the headstone. And then, with a slight stumble, moved back to face squarely the grave of his friend. As people do, when they are about to pray or to stand for a few moments' silence, their hands in front of them – always a problem, what to do with the hands – clasped just below the waist. But no, he was fumbling there, doing something, then, having accomplished it, leant back, eyes closed, or looking upwards, as he had done when they had heard the bird, and she saw it, clear as you could imagine, arching out from where his hands were, splattering over John Arlington Heigh, his wife, his children, the Peace that was Passing All Understanding, a long, golden stream – so long and so golden that, for all her horror, she couldn't help thinking of horses.

SWAN

There is at least one man who has seen it, covering the figure of the tall, pale woman who lives in the attic of the grey house on Cathedral Street near the wooden footbridge, on the eastern side of the river. A large, white bird, moving slowly, with a kind of concentrated violence. Intense. Erotic. Frightening. A glimpse of it, nothing more, as if through a light mist, although there can't have been mist in the room. Nor can he, this man, ever have been there to see. Not mist then but the veil of dream. It is not, after all, as if he knows her, or could in any way have been prepared to find himself stumbling upon them in this way, with shock – awe – in some dark corridor of one of the almost-nightmares that have been assailing him, like the sounds of people beating on a wall. A woman he has only seen four or five times, in the market or on Poets Square, near the entrance to the Alley of the Booksellers. And noticed, of course, every time: he could not deny that. A single man alone in the city, too intent on his project to contemplate a relation-ship, yet longing for one. And now he is both desperate to glimpse her again and almost afraid of doing so. To him, after so vivid a dream, it would be as if he knew her intimately. To her it would mean nothing at all. But there seems to be a law to such things. The more you want a glimpse of this kind, the less likely it is that a glimpse will occur. As if the very intensity of a desire serves to distance its object.

His book proceeds very slowly. The chapter he has been working on has taken months to compile. Each day now a few paragraphs, if he is lucky, and twice already, with the process considerably advanced, a tearing up of the draft, a beginning again, the tone, the point of view off-target, bringing him to an impasse. Writing each morning from eight until noon, then showering, dressing, going to one of the restaurants on the other side of the river, coming back through the market, shopping for his evening meal. A piece of fish sometimes at first – supposedly it was good for thought – but increasingly just cheese, bread, vegetables, the idea of dead flesh locked up and rotting inside him more and more repulsive. And now as he shops – buying vegetables, purchasing stationery, searching out a rare volume – he is looking for her, every moment, through the market, in the squares, in the Alley of the Booksellers, along River Street, along the Saint Michael Passage, along Cathedral Street. But nothing. She is nowhere. Nothing.

She becomes an obsession; *swans* become an obsession. As if they betoken her, might be a means of summoning. One day he is coming back by a different route, along the old stone galleries cut into the riverbank where the fishmongers have traditionally set up their stalls to keep their wares fresh in the warm summer months, and they are there, as he turns to mount the street-level stairs. Four of them, gleaming white on the black water, gliding majestically with the slow current, crimson-beaked, astonishing in their brightness. So that now, each day, he looks also for them, and extends his riverside walks to improve his chances. One day, on his way to interview an elderly woman in his grandfather's native village, he drives to the river marshes on the edge of the city in the vain hope that he might find them nesting there. On another he travels by bus across the city to the Royal Gardens and feeds the swans on the lake with pieces from a large pretzel he has bought at the cart by the entrance. The swans have a strange, spongy knob between and below their eyes, and some of them have raw-looking, puce-coloured bills, instead of the predominant orange. A gardener who comes over to talk to him, a short, muscular woman with bright-blue spiky hair, tells him that they are called *mute* swans. They shouldn't be eating pretzel, she says: their diet is water weed. They live on the small island in the middle of the lake. None of them are breeding pairs, she tells him. There are breeding pairs on more isolated lakes elsewhere in the country, but these are largely un-mated swans. They wander. When he tells her that he has seen them on the river near the markets, she nods and says that those are probably from this group. She asks him if he has heard the rumour – that is all it is, she says, an urban myth – of the swan that wanders the streets around the market at night. It isn't true, she says, though people keep thinking they have seen it.

One night, after a long day's work, he watches a program about Trumpeter Swans, huge birds on a vast lake in Alaska, then dreams of them taking off, lumbering into the air where they form a great V as they fly southward across the pink arctic sunset. There is something about them that seems deeply familiar, as if he might be one of them. Or perhaps it is just his loneliness, without the woman.

He is writing a biography of his grandfather, who came to live with him and his mother after the death of his father when he, the writer, was seven years old. A war hero, once a leader of partisans, his grandfather had become almost a father to him, teaching him about the forest, teaching him about birds, teaching him to garden, and so much more. Some of his earliest memories are of following him about their small plot on the edge of the city, helping him with his various chores. His grandfather's shadow, his mother used to call him, though this has come to mean something else after recent discoveries. Twenty-seven years dead now, his grandfather can no longer be asked anything, and nor can his mother, who died ten years later. If he is to find out anything it must be from the village itself, but no-one there is talking.

He has, on his desk, a photograph of his grandfather wearing a beret, rifle slung over his shoulder. A man in his early forties, virile, strong, only a few years older than the writer is now. Beside it is a photograph of his mother, taken at what must have been nearly the same time, a beautiful girl with long blonde hair, dressed in white for a church festival, her arms around her younger sisters. One of those sisters, he knows, died before the war ended. The other one her mother and her grandfather lost trace of soon afterward, and had presumed dead also. A shadow, all through his childhood, like a dark lake in the background. Beside these photographs are now photographs of swans. He wishes implausibly that he could have a photograph of the woman from the house on Cathedral Street, but knows this is absurd. For all he knows, she has moved away; indeed, she may never have existed.

Then suddenly she is there. He has just arrived at his usual restaurant, the Ifel, on the other side of the river, near the university. It is a warm late-summer day – no hint yet of autumn, though in most years it would already have shown signs of its coming – and he has taken a seat outside. Having carried a thought with him for the last hundred metres or so, he has taken out his notebook and started to write, and, looking up, the note finished, has seen her, being seated at the table opposite. She is wearing a soft-yellow blouse and light summer skirt, of an intricate Indian pattern. Her long, pale legs are bare and she is wearing light, elegant sandals. He tries to keep his eyes off her, perhaps unnecessarily since she seems quite unaware of him, but while she reads the menu he surreptitiously studies her face. She has a long slim nose, high cheekbones, eyes set so deeply that they would probably convey the impression of a tired sadness no matter what her mood. Wan, he thinks: a *wan*ness.

When his meal arrives – he has taken the daily vegetarian special so consistently that the waitress has felt no need to ask him – he eats slowly, turned slightly so that the woman is just at the edge of his vision. At one point he hears a shifting of her metal table and glances up at her more directly. She is adjusting it – one of the table legs must need bracing – and for a moment, oblivious to his watching, she parts her legs slightly as she tries to steady the table with her knee. For a few seconds – it is no more than that – he sees her inner thigh, white, secret, forbidden, and has to wrench his eyes away, in fear that she might glance up at him.

Kept at bay for months, his dream now flushes through him, like a drug suddenly released into a vein. It is all that he can do to continue his meal, for the burning consciousness of her proximity. Her own meal, meanwhile, arrives, is eaten, paid for. When she leaves he watches her walk westward along the riverbank and then he rises, pays for his own meal, and walks off quickly in the opposite direction. Forsaking his daily market visit – he can do that later – he goes directly to his apartment and into its tiny bathroom. Closing the door, not turning on the light, he braces himself against the wall, in total darkness, and masturbates, more rapidly and violently than he has done in years.

It is weeks later. He has not seen her. Again she seems to have disappeared. The weather is closing in. People are now wearing overcoats, scarves, heavy sweaters. Although a few of the cafés and restaurants still have outdoor tables, they are for the braver clients who either want to be seen or to take advantage of the occasional outbreaks of sun. Evening comes earlier. He is in the local delicatessen for bread and wine and olives when he hears two elderly ladies by the cheese counter talking quietly about a swan. He pretends to be looking for cheese himself, in order to listen more closely. They are speaking of a third, a friend, Vladka, who has seen something in the Bishop's lane, hard by the cathedral.

'The one with the mushroom sellers?' asks one.

'No,' says the other, 'that little alleyway that runs off it, near the Bible shop, and slopes down to the river.'

Nor is it clear whether what Vladka saw was the swan at all – that, the word that had initially caught his attention, was merely the first reaction of the smaller of these two women, when the other had mentioned it – but it was large, and feathered, or appeared to be, in a very dark part of the alley, an alcove, near some rubbish bins. She had only glimpsed it, Vladka, when someone had opened a door to let out a cat; it might just have been a bundle of rags, but she could have sworn.

'Did she try to touch it, poke it with her stick?' the smaller woman asks.

'No! Of course not,' says the other. 'Imagine if it had moved! Hissed at her! She would probably have fallen and broken something.'

'And it might have been a person after all, a man, trying to sleep.'

'Yes, a man, and he wouldn't have taken kindly to being poked with a stick!'

Back in the apartment, hours later, his dinner over and his bottle of wine half-finished, he washes the dishes and, turning out the kitchen light, about to go back to his desk, looks out the window at the moon rising above the hill behind the house. It is a clear night. He can even see a few stars. And, hearing one of his neighbours coming slowly up the ancient stairs from the street below, resolves something. Rummaging in the cupboard beneath the kitchen bench he locates his torch, checks it, changes its batteries and sets out for the Bishop's lane. He is there within minutes, at first walking its length, trying to accustom himself to the pitch dark, then retracing his steps, using the torch carefully, keeping its beam on the ground close by him, aware that whoever lives in these houses – priests, most of them – may not take kindly to someone searching their alleyway. But, although he finds three or four likely alcoves, a couple of them with bins in them, there is nothing untoward. No pile of rags, no homeless person trying to sleep, no swan.

The idea, however, stays with him. The next day he must go back to his grandfather's village. A lead has opened; there is someone who might be willing to talk. As he drives – it is almost two hours away – he finds himself counting up how many such alleys there are in the old part of the city. He can think of at least eleven, on either side of the river, and certainly there are more; alleys, and some ancient cobbled arcades, with darker and more likely spaces even than the alcoves he had found in the Bishop's lane. He decides to search them all, if only to convince himself that there is nothing.

As he drives back, he is frustrated but also more hopeful about his project than usual, since although this person has claimed they know nothing, they have told him of a man in another village who had been a young partisan in his grandfather's brigade. Rain begins to fall, light at first but eventually torrential. It sets in for days. There is no possibility, until it thoroughly clears, that any creature would think to forage, let alone sleep in the alleys. Yet the idea of them nags at him, seems to want to draw him in. It is a week before he can explore the first of them, and a month before he has visited them all, and by that time he has long realised that the process is much more complicated than he had envisioned. Why should the swan, if the swan exists, stay in one place? What is to say that at one time it is not in an alley not yet visited, and at another in an alley he has searched already?

When the winter nights allow, he begins to go through them again – the alleys, the lanes, the impasses – and to visit them randomly. Not every night, and sometimes not for a week or more. He comes to think of it more as an evening walk than as a search. He is *drawn to* it, he would probably say, if there were ever anyone to ask him; it is not even something that he has consciously chosen. Some nights he does not bother to take a torch. On one such night he is walking slowly through a lane that has become quite familiar to him. Though cobbled and as ancient as any, it is a little wider than most, with an arcade along one of its sides, and towards the centre a section of it built in overhead so that it becomes, for six or seven metres, a kind of tunnel. He has just come through this section when he senses – it is senses, rather than sees – something in a dark passageway, a space barely a shoulder's width wide, off to his right. He has just decided that it can have been no more than a cat, or a large rat, and turned to resume his progress when a door opens a few metres ahead to the left and someone comes out, caught briefly in silhouette in the sudden light from a stairway. He steps back into the narrow passage, not wanting to be seen, knowing how disturbing some might find it to encounter a stranger in their alley at this time. A small, curtained window opposite him is throwing a little light into the alley, barely sufficient to see his own hand by. As the figure passes, however, he can make out enough, and the racing in his chest, a kind of giddiness, confirms it. It is her.

The next day, on the way to his lunch, he goes back to find the door. There is a plaque beside it and a picture of a broad white beach. A travel agency. Perhaps she is employed there. Perhaps, the evening before, she had been working late. He goes up the stairs to a small landing. A door to the left, a door to the right, and before him the door to the agency. He knocks and, when there is no response, turns the handle and walks in. A small, cluttered office. A thin, bald man with round, wire-rimmed glasses and a drooping moustache, and a gum-chewing secretary with lank blonde hair and an acned face, each of them looking so bemused they might have forgotten what a customer looks like. He asks them – it is the first thing that comes to his mind – about airfares to Thailand. They cannot help him. They deal only with eastern Europe. The beach, he calculates, as he walks back down the stairs, must be somewhere on the Black Sea. And clearly she does not work there. Perhaps she lives or works behind one of the other doors. Or has a friend there. Or lover. Unless he watches the place – and that for the moment seems impossible – he will never know.

He changes his lunch-hour walk and for a time passes through the lane almost daily, but never sees her. His book is drawing towards an end; at least, his most difficult chapters are. Hopefully the rest will recompose itself around them. The person in the other village – it was in fact a hospice, and the man, although eighty-five and clearly dying, had a lucid memory and was anxious to unburden himself – had told him more than enough. The old man had been just twenty when the war ended, a partisan for almost three years; and his, the writer's, grand-father had been the leader of the local brigade. When the war finished the man had thought the brigade's work over but it was clear that it wasn't. For weeks after the Germans had withdrawn there had been a steady flow of collaborators following them, in fear of their lives, and now, with the fighting over and the neighbouring countries refusing to harbour them, there began a steady flow back. Contingents, in forced marches. The collaborators who found themselves forcibly returned to the villages in their area had had a nasty time of it. There were beatings, murders, executions, rapes. From leading the local fight against the occupiers, his grandfather and those men under him who were prepared to help, found themselves in a peacekeeping role, trying to hold back a flood of fury and revenge. And it hadn't just been locals forced to return. There had been others, passing through, on their way to the next border. A miserable lot, going back as some of them were – for some had worked in extermination camps – to almost certain death.

The brigade was part of a system of safe passage. They would meet another brigade, from villages to the west, and a party of repatriants would be handed over. They would take them through the woods, avoiding the villages themselves, where things could get out of hand, and would hand their charges over to the next brigade a few kilometres to the east. They had done this four times already, but there was something different about the fifth group. Maybe it was because there was some particular person in it, or maybe there was some change of policy: he had not been told. They took them to an old mine entrance, high up along the ridges, that they had used to rest the earlier groups, under guard. As before, they had fed them, issued them blankets and straw and lamps and locked them in behind the huge wooden doors that had been put in place when the mine closed. Only this time – it was a group of almost twenty, men mainly but a few women, a couple of the men and women quite elderly – his grandfather had ordered them to brick the entrance closed. Not straight away. At first they had gone to a nearby village for a meeting, and for some food of their own; but then they had gone back and done the brickwork by torchlight. He, the man in the nursing home, had only done what he was told; others – there were seven of them altogether – had seemed to follow the orders without question, and so he had done likewise.

It had been eerily silent behind the wooden doors as they worked. As if everyone within were too deeply asleep to hear. When they had finished they had gone back down to the village and behaved as normal. As far as anyone else knew they had passed this group on to the next brigade just as they had the others. And no-one had spoken. There had been an unvoiced understanding that no-one would ever talk about it, and no-one had. But now that the bones had been found, now that the other partisans were all dead, and the old man himself as good as dead, he could tell it all at last. Whether his grandfather had done it on his own initiative, however, or whether he was following orders from elsewhere, he could not or would not say. The old man had always assumed it was the latter. One of the other partisans, after a long night of drinking, twenty years afterwards, when they had spoken about that eerie silence, had said something about strychnine in the food: that they had been taken away for their 'meeting' so that they couldn't hear the screaming, the hammering on the wood. But who knows? Perhaps, after all, that would have been the kindest way. The old man has had dreams, he tells the writer, all his life since, terrible dreams.

It is a grey day. The bells have woken him again. The Angelus. Normally he can sleep through it, or at least go back to sleep, but there are mornings, and it seems this is one of them, when he knows that that will be impossible. He must, in any case, write. He is just a sentence away from the end of this most difficult chapter, and he should type it while it is clear in his mind. He gets up and, beginning to dress, looks back at the bedsheets and the strange, bird-like shape that has formed itself among them – almost expected by now, almost familiar – and wonders if he will ever know how it gets there, ever know what it means.

A TRAVELLER'S TALE

Some stories float in time and space, unattached to anything. You know the kind: *There once was a man, a traveller, who set out on a long journey ...* I want you to think about that. A voice *tells* these stories to you the reader, but that voice says nothing about itself, tells you nothing of the teller or even why the story is being told in the first place, apart from the fact that it seems to be assumed that it is a good and interesting and entertaining thing to do. Instead, the story floats in a bubble of time that moves, as if hermetically sealed, from time *to* time as it is told and retold, in a bubble of space that is sealed in the same way.

Space that is no space. Time that is no time. I want you to think about that, too. I want you to think about it because I am conscious that this story might in some ways, at some points, seem like that. Perhaps inevitably. And I want you to know that, if it does, it is not because the events upon which the story is based – the events which inspired the story, or perhaps it would be better to say *threw off* the story, as a cicada leaves behind its carapace or a snake a skin it has outgrown – occurred in some timeless time or placeless place. Sometimes the teller does not say anything about themselves because they cannot. Sometimes the story is not being told because it is a good or an entertaining thing. Sometimes the story is being told because it has to be.

I don't know why I have written that paragraph. It was not my intention to do so. There's a nervousness when you are about to begin a long story – to begin to spin it, as it were, from all the fibres that have gathered about you, some of which you have gathered yourself, and others of which have come like nocturnal creatures drawn by the light of a fire. It's as if an older person were about to set out on a long journey and they don't know if they have quite the strength to do it, if their legs will carry them all that way, if the terrain or the weather will be too much for them. They don't know what the politics are going to be like, let's say, or the bureaucracy – whether they will be held up at borders, or ambushed on country roads, or waylaid in strange streets in strange towns by officers of ambiguous allegiance demanding papers that they do not have. A nervousness *like* that, anyway, if not quite that. One sits there, with the paper and the pen, or perhaps the computer screen in front of one, and like that traveller one checks one's pockets to make sure that one has one's wallet, one's passport, one's pills, one's keys; looks around one, checks again for the map, the toiletries, the changes of clothes; looks out at the weather, goes, mentally, one more time through the checklist of the things one does in order to enable oneself to depart.

Normally, of course, this is all removed from the narrative that the reader encounters. But for some reason – something instinctual, I can't really say much more about it than that – I can't yet erase them, indeed I think that, for once, just this once, perhaps I shouldn't. The journey, *this* journey, is too important. The *heart* is too involved. And when I say the heart, of course, I'm not sure that I'll be understood – well, no, what I mean to say is that, *to* be understood, I feel that I need to explain that what I have in mind when I say *the heart* is a very durable thing that stretches over a whole lifetime, that is one of the most stressed and yet most constant, toughest, most *durable* organs of the body; the heart that has to get up in the morning and take up the often heavy – often very heavy, often *too* heavy – burden of being, let's call it, and carry it, somehow, to the day's other end. Even though it might just have been 'broken'; even though it might just been stretched, or laden beyond measure. But that is of course not only the bodily organ but also the metaphor, for the supposed centre and origin of love, for example, though of course not only of love – for tenacity, too, and other things are involved: courage, let's say, or generosity. The heart that is, in the human mind, heart-*shaped*. The heart that is in so many ways also so vulnerable, that one also seeks to protect. So that the heart that I speak of – *write* of – here, is, as the heart has to be, as it can only be, a mixture, an amalgam of the two, of the bodily and the metaphoric hearts, as if they could ever be separated.

When one seeks to speak honestly (of course one cannot say *speaks* honestly, but only *seeks* to speak honestly, do you see?) one slows down, and has to grope through the words, like coming down a mountain path at dusk, having to choose each step most carefully, since the early dew has made the rocks slippery, since the gravel is unstable, since there are roots protruding that are hard to see in the half-light.

That nervousness then, because the heart is involved. And because the ruggedness of the terrain one is about to attempt one's journey through is also in some measure the country *of*, the terrain *of*, the heart. But enough. There is too much of this already. I must apologise. (But then the reader does not know, cannot yet know, how much the heart is involved!) I think, nonetheless, that I have brought myself to the door, as it were, and am ready to open it, to step out, although not without registering the small irony that the first thing one does after stepping out, after crossing the threshold, is to turn around and to face the door, either to lock it or to check that it has locked itself, just as, from the gate, it is likely that one will turn and look at the house itself – to see that the curtains are drawn, that there is no longer any smoke from the chimney – as at something, some beloved thing, that one might never see again. Even then, having checked that the door is locked and turned again to face the journey in front of one, it is not always quite so simple – one's next move is not always quite so simple – as my metaphor, my allegory, might have seemed to suggest. In a real journey, even if it is going to be a journey of many thousands of kilometres, one would presumably, having stepped through the door, having crossed the threshold, know where to go. Down the path, let's say, or the driveway, and turn left, towards the road, and then, at the road, turn right and walk towards the village or the highway, go down into the valley or up towards the mountain pass, or head out over the plain. But with a story, a long narrative, it is not always so easy. The paths diverge in the wood, let's say, or other paths enter them. One comes over and over to crossroads and the choice is not clear. Many roads lead to one's destination; many roads prevent one from getting there.

One has, perhaps – for example – learnt of the importance of the narrative, come to realise, as indeed is the case here, that the story is a story that *has* to be told, only because one has come to an end of it (do you see that I say *an* end, not *the* end? a whole extra complication there, in this matter of beginnings and endings; how they don't exist, for the most part, or how they only exist in story, how their existence is perhaps one of the ways of telling that a story *is* a story). And if one has come to understand the importance of a story because one has encountered the end of it, *an* end of it – because one has encountered, found oneself involved in, the horror or tragedy of it, the *damage*, let's call it, because that is what it is after all, great damage, although in this instance the tough, worn heart has been able to deal with it, *is* dealing with it – if that is what one has encountered, and is what has convinced one that the story is so important in the first place, then the ending, *that* ending, may in fact be the beginning, if not of the story itself then of the need to be telling it, and perhaps therefore should be in some way the beginning of that telling. Although in truth – I skipped over it just now, because involved with another trajectory, but even as I did the skipping over I knew that that was what I was doing and that I would have to go back to it – one cannot ignore or allow to pass unremarked this matter of the complication of beginnings and endings. Things *continue past* 'endings', even and perhaps especially things deeply involved *in* those endings. The heart, let's say – but I have already said this – has to get up the next day. People have to live with those endings, and the consequences of those endings.

And it's not just endings. Begin with a beginning, *look* at it, and you know, of course, that it's not really or only a beginning. The traveller seen in his cottage at the beginning of this story, for example, was already fifty-eight years old – such a life lived, to get there! – and in even the most confined limits of that cottage and that morning had risen, after what kind of sleep, with what apprehensions, what memories going through his mind? What fears, what expectations, what dreams of resolution, of peace, at last, upon the eventual conclusion of the journey he was only just about to begin?

Nor, of course, is it a matter of him alone. How could it be? Nor of – *only* of – that other party – of her – whose damage he is setting out to tell, whose damage, indeed, is still unrolling and revealing itself even as he sets out to tell of it. No (and there is another fork in the road there, another thing being skipped over;

I am well aware of it: the way that the thing being told can be changing even as the telling is progressing, that *the telling changes the told*, that the told abandons, diverges from the telling, sometimes leaving the telling wrong footed – that there is this *radical discordance* of processes). No. For there are, of course, in almost any story, other parties involved. At the beginning of a story, let's say, there is a moment – hence this *nervousness*; I am back at this *nervousness* again – when, as at the beginning of a parade, all of the participants in that parade, the walking participants, the participants on floats, the drivers of the trucks beneath those floats, the marching bands, the dancers and the acrobats, gather in a marshalling area and either sort out, or are given instructions by someone, an author, as to who will go out in which order. And, of course, everyone in that marshalling area has come from somewhere. Every one *has journeyed* to the 'beginning' of the story, even those who will seem only to transect it at some point deep into its progress. Have journeyed, to the beginning, from their own beginnings, and the beginnings of those beginnings.

But here I am, at the door, at last, and although the nervousness has not fully been dealt with, has not been overcome, at least it has been addressed, *suggested*, the traveller realising, as it were, that there can be no complete preparation, no absolute assurance that he is ready, and that there comes a moment, there *must* come a moment, when one simply *declares* so, or *assumes* so, and departs or commences one's departure – steps out, as it were – and ah, that is a source of nervousness again, the *territory*, the *jaggedness of the ground* – into the wide world, the difficult terrain, of this horrid, distressing, almost-untellable tale.

THE PANTHER

I came across the panther in the National Gallery, in a painting entitled *Bestiary* by a little-known French artist of the late eighteenth century, Auguste Lorrain. I remember thinking how ordinary the painting was and wondering why anyone would have wanted to enshrine it at all, until I saw it there, the panther, in the shadows at the back, seeming to stare – no, I will say *staring* – directly at me, its eyes so piercing they seemed to be tracking my thought itself. I mumbled something and my companion, leaning towards me, asked what I had said. 'Nothing,' I replied, 'nothing,' and then, in afterthought, 'Why do you think it is, whenever artists are doing compositions of this kind – you know, all these Temptations of Saint Anthony and the like – that they have to put in there, a *panther*?' My friend looked at me, then at the painting, quite closely, and then at me again, and at last, a quizzical look on his face, shrugged. Only later did it occur to me that he had probably not seen the panther at all.

We went out for a drink afterwards, and talked about other things. After two glasses of wine and a long discussion about the coming election I suggested we go off to dinner somewhere, but he, a married man, was due home and so we parted on the pavement outside and I walked back towards my own small, book-crowded house through the old quarter, pausing over the curiosities in the boutique windows, and out, down Republic Avenue, along the edge of the National Gardens.

It was only then, away from the lights of the restaurants and cafés and the congenial congestion of the narrow streets, that I began to get the feeling that, although I could see no other pedestrian within fifty metres before or behind me, I was not alone. I stopped and peered into the shadows of the Gardens, listening intently, but could see or hear nothing. Twenty metres further on, the feeling continuing, I stopped, repeated my survey, and decided to cross to the other side of the avenue where the lighting was better and there were more people about. I do not carry much money but the little I do is hard-earned and I don't much fancy being mugged for it. Five minutes later, at my door, I paused and looked back before entering. It was a warm night. Bats were already darting about the streetlights. Apart from an elderly man putting out garbage on the other side of the road, there seemed to be nobody around.

Inside, I poured myself another glass of wine and began to think about food. There was little in the pantry – I should have been shopping rather than at the gallery – but within a few minutes I had the makings of a pasta with onions, garlic, olives, crushed dried pepper and some of the fine, rich oil I bring with me from my sister's neighbour in the country. I then set to opening my mail and had just shuffled through the half-dozen envelopes – bank statements, bills, charities asking for money, a letter from my publisher doubtless telling me how poorly my books were selling – when I heard a muted thud in my courtyard. A burglar, I thought immediately, and my heart raced as I stepped back into a small alcove by the telephone, from which I could watch the French doors – thankfully locked – without being observed.

A shadow moved there, black against the night's blackness, too low to be human, unless this burglar had injured himself in his drop from the wall, or was accustomed to approaching on all fours. A cat, I thought, but this was far too big. A large dog? But dogs do not leap walls. And what could it want? And then I saw the eyes. Exactly as they had been in the gallery. Absurd. Impossible. Electrifying. My first inclination was to think, in some embarrassment, that I was losing my mind. I looked away, a reflex action, and then back again, to find them thankfully vanished – the eyes and the shadow both.

Not *wanting* to see them, I suppose, I turned and got on with my dinner, reflecting upon the matter as I ate. If I had been dreaming then the dream had a remarkable realism and intensity. And as to my mind, well, it had not as yet shown any other signs of deterioration. But perhaps one could not oneself be always the best judge. Clearly it would be better to investigate than to ignore the issue. My meal over, I took my plate into the kitchen, came back and bent down, looked more closely through the door-glass into the darkness. Nothing. At first. Nothing. But then I looked up. The tree. There is a large tree on the other side of the courtyard, an old plane tree, with strong lower branches, upon one of which a panther was stretched out, staring into me. As if it had been waiting for a signal it now rose, leapt down – that quiet thud again – and ambled across the flagstones.

It seemed that there was little to do but open the door and allow the creature ingress. Strangely the prospect did not strike me with fear. Rather I had a feeling – an impression – of patience and calm expectation, on both sides. As if it already knew the place it walked in, without hurry or hesitation, looking about itself, taking the scent of things at leisure. Having visited the kitchen, the hall, my study, it came back to the living room and took possession of the sofa. Was this dream? Was this insanity? I simply did not know. I sat two hours watching it, and for the most part being watched in return. I had no idea what it was thinking. Eventually, bored or satisfied, it closed its eyes and to all appearances went to sleep. Having in my kitchen no milk or meat, for I do not consume such things, I got for it a large bowl of water, deferring until daylight the question of sustenance. Who knew? If this was all a dream the matter might never arise. Seeing no point in sitting down there again, and feeling too exhilarated for sleep, I went to my study and wrote my diary. A test. In the morning, with any luck, there would be no panther, no bowl of water, nothing written under this day's date.

And indeed in the morning the creature was gone, although only half of the water, and none of my curious entry concerning the events of the night before. How it contrived to open the door I do not know, but then I was never to know, in the year thereafter. It never left while I was there, did not often arrive while I was there. Simply it *was*, on the sofa, or on the arrangement of cushions and blankets that I set up for it in my study. Thankfully it showed – but I should not call it 'it', since it was very definitely a 'he' – no interest in following me up to my bed.

Nor was there any knowing when he would be there or not. Sometimes he was with me several evenings in a row; sometimes gone for a week. Where he went when he was not with me I cannot say. Perhaps out into the countryside. Perhaps to some other abode. Perhaps back to the gallery, up into the painting again. Once, in the early months, upon a whim, not having seen him for forty-eight hours or more, I went back there to see. His eyes were there, as on that first day, staring, with only the slightest hint of recognition – the trace of a trace – although I readily admit that even this may have been my imagination. On another occasion, when he'd been almost ten days away, he met me at the National Gardens as I was walking home after dinner with a friend, if a meeting it was to realise that he was accompanying me, in the first tier of shadows, scarcely more than a rustling amongst them, the glint of his eyes now there and now not as he passed beneath the branches. Indeed I put the beginning of our walks, our night perambulations, down to this night, for it can't have been long afterward that, tiring of my writing, I went out to walk at midnight, on a night when he was not with me, only to find him, now following and now keeping pace, padding from tree to tree through the suburb as if it was as familiar to him as to me.

I'd become complacent, by this. In the first month I'd done little else but interrogate the relationship almost obsessively in the attempt to determine what kind of being he was, even the extent to which he could be said to be being at all, but with our growing familiarity this had passed. On one such late-evening walk, however, we encountered an acquaintance, approaching so directly that there was no means of avoiding him. I was surprised that my panther did not recede into the shadows, melt strategically away. Instead, while I spoke with this gentleman, a librarian, the panther sat, half in shadow, I'll admit, but so close to heel that I could only presume that my acquaintance quite simply could not see him.

In time these night walks came to mean a lot to me. We would go into the vast Gardens – a place one is still well advised to stay away from after dark – and I became reacquainted with the peace and strangeness there, and the people and creatures who constitute its community of shadows. Drunks. Prostitutes going about their business. Night searchers. Nyctophiles. Once, uncannily, a deer grazing, for whom I immediately feared, only to find that it seemed to know and was not in any way alarmed by my companion. Once an old, great-bearded man who spoke in the strange phrases of a visionary. And, more than once, in the open space by the derelict rotunda, which seemed a kind of chapel to her, a bruised but beautiful young woman, in rags, who seemed to me to be somehow intellectually impaired, but who spoke each time with the panther dearly and softly, as if with an old friend, cradling his head in her hands, holding it to her breast, draping her long silver hair over him, with a tenderness I would suddenly long for.

Now and again, too, other of these night people would speak to us, or so it seemed, or shout, in their dark-shrouded anger or drunkenness. Once a bottle was thrown, he did not flinch; and once a couple were fucking in a broad space of moonlight and he padded over to them, investigated them intimately – surely they felt his hot breath! – then lay only a pace away, staring as if awaiting the moment to devour. And as we left the Gardens, as often as not, there would be an encounter with the amputee who kept vigil from a bench by the entrance, either welcoming or abusing us, depending upon the state of his inebriation, at one time, to my alarm, roaring that the panther had taken his leg, though this proved to be a joke, for there was laughter as we walked away.

On one of the earliest of these night walks, on the far side of the Gardens, my companion disappeared down a lane. The question of food had preoccupied me for a time, until I realised that it seemed no part of what he expected of me. I assumed that he looked after this himself – that someone else was feeding him, perhaps – and that a belly recently filled was one of the reasons he would go to sleep so quickly after reclaiming his couch. Or perhaps, so strange a being as this being was, he had no need of food at all. But now, as if to tell me something – but what was it? – he reappeared with a parcel in his mouth and laid it carefully at my feet. Of meat, packaged for a supermarket and thrown away, having been tainted somehow, or passed its expiry date. It seemed he was asking me to unwrap it, which I did, with little pleasure, the first time I had touched meat in years.

The speed with which he then consumed the contents was disconcerting and the sight most unpleasant, of and in itself but also because he seemed to hate what he was doing; but I must admit that it gave me an idea, and on several occasions thereafter, recollecting, I investigated late at night a butcher's or a supermarket bin and brought home things I found there. The idea of eating the flesh of a living creature is abhorrent to me, but so too is the thought that, once its life has been taken so hideously, any portion of its sacred body should suffer the further indignity of being discarded – a logic, I'll admit, so fraught with its own inconsistencies that I'm glad only the panther has ever had to keep my secret.

Towards the end of the summer I went, as always, to visit my sister in the village. Normally I would go for a few days every month or two – she is a painter, and we enjoy each other's company – but for several months I'd not done so, reluctant to abandon my visitor, and despite the protests of my sister, to whom I could offer no satisfactory explanation. I could not avoid my annual sojourn, however, and so it was that I locked up my narrow city house and departed, apprehensive as I was that it might spell an end to this strange relationship.

I need not have worried. It was less than a week before he found me. I was sitting out with my sister one evening, drinking a last glass of wine with her in her large garden, when I became conscious of his eyes, staring from under the oleander, out of my sister's line of sight. It was possible that she might be one of those who would not see him, but she and I are so intimate, in so many ways, that I had little confidence of this. In the city I live reclusively, within the confines of my house, largely unobserved, but that was not the case here. Even if she could not see the panther – but he seemed to *choose* who would see him – it would be hard for me to behave as if he were not there.

'You know,' I said, slowly, after a break in our conversation, the panther's eyes appearing to urge me to continue, 'that I have been absorbed, lately – preoccupied – in town …'

'Yes,' she said, leaning in a little, encouraging. She wanted me to have a partner, a lover, and I imagined she thought I was about to tell her of one. But as I went on, explaining everything, expecting, even from her, nothing but alarm and incredulity, I found only wide-eyed intrigue.

'But I know!' she said at last, 'I have seen him! The day after you came. In the orchard, near the barn. I am so glad! I thought I was losing my mind!' And then, after a pause, as if sensing, suddenly, its presence, 'But why do you bring this up now?' And I told her, instructed her, to look around calmly, with no sudden movement, into the shadow beneath the dark bushes with their moon-pale flowers.

In retrospect I see it as a turning-point, that moment in the garden. We managed the next two weeks quite well. The panther was an almost constant presence, and now that he had made my sister's acquaintance – clearly the thing he had been seeking that evening – a presence much closer to the house, although, oddly, he never sought to enter. And, when I returned to the city, within hours he was there.

It was some time in the third week of September that I heard from my sister, a phone call in which, for several minutes, she seemed uncharacteristically to avoid coming to her point. Eventually, however, she asked about 'my' panther, and I described how swiftly he had made his way back, and how easily we'd resumed our urban routine, our midnight walks, our forays into the National Gardens.

There were two things she wanted to tell me. The first she recounted with some amusement, albeit an amusement unusually brittle. One of the villagers, a drunkard named Anton, had evidently seen the panther one night when we were there, and had been muttering about it ever since. No-one was taking him seriously and she would not have thought it worth mentioning had it not been for a piece she had just come upon in the local newspaper. Some sheep in a nearby village had been killed during the time we were there. Attacked and partly devoured by some other animal or animals. The attacks were being attributed to a pack of dogs seen in the area over recent months. It probably *was* the dogs, she assured me, and I readily agreed, but she was nervous that someone, perhaps Anton himself, might make a different connection. At least one other, according to Anton, had seen the panther, or been told by another that *they* had seen a panther, and although this was unverified it seemed to suggest that a rumour was spreading.

'Like an urban myth,' I commented, 'or a rural version of one'.

'Yes,' she said, 'and let's hope people treat it as such'.

I smiled to myself as I recounted the story to the panther – who eyed me quizzically the whole time, as if recognising something pertaining to himself, but then closed his eyes, unfazed, and returned to his dreaming – and then, I think, after a period of reflection concerning any lessons there might be for our own night wanderings, I rather forgot about the matter. Certainly there were people who had seen him – and seen him with me – but there seemed so far to have been almost a benign conspiracy to say nothing. No-one in my non-panther life had mentioned him, let alone any rumour of a panther at large in the city. It was not, after all, as if the city was without its own mythic bestiary: the alligators that supposedly inhabited the sewerage system, dogs the size of ponies that lived in the bowels of the disused abattoirs, vampire bats that flew out on moonless nights from the old hospital incinerator tower.

Our life together was our own, it seemed to me, all the more private and carefully guarded as our relationship developed. I appeared to draw something human out of him, or answered to it, and he, who knows?, drew something panther-like from me – became, in the longer and longer nights of winter, a kind of witness to my loneliness, my secrets, and, yes, for I *was* a man alone, an angered man, an embarrassed man, my furies, my disappointments, my desires, my confessions. And he seemed to swallow them, even in some way to understand. Although the season was rapidly cooling, we would still go, some nights, to visit the National Gardens, and on others wander the deserted streets and laneways, farther and farther from home. And on other nights, he, I, would go out to prowl alone. I fed him on dreams, I fed him on disgust. I fed him on all the horrors and pornographies of this human world. What in return he was trying to instil in me, with those slow-burning, emerald-yellow eyes, that infinite patience, I will never truly know.

~

The first of the murders occurred in late autumn. Murders, killings: I didn't know. A homeless man in a small park by the river. I thought little of it. Such killings, always heinous, are sadly never uncommon. And the detail escaped me, if any had been given at all. It was out of our way; we had never been to the river together, let alone the culvert by the roadside there where homeless people would shelter on inclement nights. Nor did I think too much about the second – although I did raise my eyes at it, and read about it to my companion – of a young man, a drug addict, in the very lane from which I had been brought the packaged meat those several months before.

It can't have been much after this, a fortnight perhaps, time just enough for me to make no immediate association, that I read the first unconfirmed account of the sighting of a large black cat in the vicinity of the National Gardens. A discussion ensued amongst various editorial correspondents, during which other glimpses were reported, earlier such stories remembered, and even an account recalled from almost ninety years before of a panther kept as a pet by a resident of the quarter, a retired general from one of the Central American republics who had reputedly used the creature in his tortures there. Word was spreading, or rather an idea; it seemed only a matter of time before the stories of the murders – there was a third, which seemed to me quite unrelated, but alarm was catching – and those of the panther collided. My companion was with me every bit as much as he had been, and I had never known any violence in him, but I felt, nonetheless, a bleak apprehension germinate within me, like the seed of a rank and poisonous weed.

It was the next murder, the fourth, that unleashed the storm. A sudden, terrible thought came to me as I read of it. The young woman with the silver hair, in the National Gardens, very near where we had been used to meeting her. Murdered most viciously, for, for the first time, the police were releasing details, making connections. These killings, for they now called them that, appeared to have been done by some great cat. There were claw patterns, deep lacerations at the neck of the victims that could only have been made by large, powerful jaws. The sightings of the jaguar, they had reluctantly concluded – jaguar, or puma, or panther – had been actual, no illusion, and it was this beast they now searched for. They urged people to exercise the greatest vigilance in the area, to report anything, however minor, that might seem related, and at the same time warned us strongly against taking this matter into our own hands. Already vigilante groups had formed, and the police were working to discourage them. Experts were being consulted. Tissue analyses were underway. The situation would shortly be under control.

And of course I doubted him, more than doubted. How could I not? And began to fear. The evidence was overwhelming. The sheep in the village near my sister's. His night prowlings. The claw pattern. And the girl – that, of all things; that it should be *her* – seemed to my abyssal confusion as damning as it was unthinkable. But how could I betray him? It would have been easy, but I could not bring myself to do it. And yet by the same token it was impossible to keep him with me. People *had* seen us together. It was only a matter of time, days, perhaps hours, before one of these reported us. And if he had turned upon *her*, how could I be sure that he would not turn upon me? Neither of us was safe while he was there. Nor could I escape with him. I could only expel him somehow, evict him, and hope that no others, himself included, would lose their lives as a consequence.

The night immediately following the report of the girl's murder I took advantage of his absence to lock the French doors and – something I'd not done since he arrived, but I thought it might convey a message – draw the thick curtains across them. I felt soon his heavy drop to the courtyard, felt his presence on the other side of the glass, felt, like a physical ache, his eyes as they attempted to pierce the fabric, but did nothing. And on the third day, for it took that long, felt – knew, clearly – that he had gone.

For the next two weeks I scoured the papers and listened regularly to the news for further sightings but none were reported. And no further murders. There were now several vigilante groups roaming the night streets armed with sticks, knives, guns, drinking as they went, primed with their drugs of choice, urgent for an encounter, and the city itself was fixated upon the issue, but there was nothing, no sign. I went out only during daylight, and by routes as far from the Gardens as I could. Whenever I arrived home I expected police at my door. But in fact all was suddenly, eerily silent. Until the fifteenth night, when, shortly after twelve, a pounding on my street door flooded me with a sense of imminent disaster.

It was the one-legged man from the Gardens entrance. 'Come!' he said, nothing more, but from the look in his eyes I knew I had no choice. Immediately I followed, without so much as locking the door, scarcely believing how swiftly he travelled, his crutches pounding onto the pavement, his body swinging through the arc of them, crutches thrust forward and pounding again. In almost no time we were past the entrance and into the dark paths, heading – how was I so sure of it? – towards the clearing by the rotunda.

The howl that came from me as I saw him there even now wakes me, on the worst of nights, as if in a vain attempt to spare me the agony of that last stare, or the loathsome, heart-rending image they had made of him, strung up between the posts at the top of the rotunda stairs, arrows from a crossbow in his side and neck, a piece of wood strapped into his mouth, exposed to their hideous version of the death of the thousand cuts, his sleek fur matted and glistening with blood. I flung myself towards him but some powerful brute grabbed my arm and threw me to the ground, landing at the same time – or was this someone else? – a heavy blow on the back of my skull, as if to bring me instant, almost merciful darkness.

I woke at dawn on the cripple's bench, stinking of alcohol, my head pounding, the ragged ends of a horrid dream clinging to my mind like the remains of someone's excrement. At first I had no sense of where I was or how I had come to be there, but all too quickly it came back. I vomited, between my legs, then staggered to my feet and made my way to the clearing. Nothing. No corpse. No stain between the posts of the rotunda. Nothing. Until, prompted by some heavy rancidness in the air, I fell to my knees, pulled away some rotten boards and crawled under, to see the spooled blood still only partly congealed, felt my hands, my knees in the pool of it.

I sobbed alone there, a long while, but then, coming to myself, realising that I could not risk being seen like that, washed myself as best I could in the duck pond nearby, and made my way home, or rather found myself there, the memory of how I reached it submerged in the questions overwhelming me. How could he have allowed himself to be caught like that? How could it have been that he could not fight them off? How could he have done what he had done? How *could* it have been *he*?

For weeks I was in a stupor. Slept heavily. Drank heavily. Could not work. Correspondence piled up in the hallway. Newspapers were dumped unread by the door. Until eventually there was a headline I could not ignore. Another murder, with the same profile, the same horrid wounds. A nurse, on her way home from a late shift at the Women's Hospital. The panther, again, but not *that* panther, not *my* panther, surely. And I experienced a gruesome re-awakening. Was he still here? Alive and dead at the same time? Had that been him? Had I – it was only now that the chilling possibility occurred to me – been living in the same house in which that general had once lived?

I had all but resolved, in extremis, to take my bizarre, scarcely credible story to the police – to sacrifice *myself*, if that is what it meant – when a further headline arrived, blaring and triumphant. 'The Panther', for so they now dubbed him, had been caught, a young fitter and turner who worked in a prestige machine-shop on the edge of the city, making custom parts for classic cars. A lone sociopath, obsessed with big cats, who had fashioned for himself an artificial claw – a gruesome photograph was provided – with which to disfigure his victims after he had at first beaten and then throttled them, paying particular attention to their throats to cover signs of their strangulation.

That is thirty years ago. And now, hotly discussed, there is talk of his release. The whole matter stirs again. And I am still alone, still in the same house, still writing, almost seventy. Lingering, for reasons I can't explain. I have my admirers, as I have always had, but am in most common respects quite unsuccessful. Those critics who pay my books any attention say almost to a person that they are beautifully written, even haunting, but that there is always some indefinable thing missing, an unspoken absence around which everything turns. Every year, in late summer, I visit my sister, who also remains alone. And every year, in autumn, I go to the Art Gallery, to stand before *Bestiary*.

I can see him, there in the shadows.

He never looks at me.

THE AUTHOR WOULD LIKE TO ACKNOWLEDGE

THE FOLLOWING PRIOR PUBLICATIONS:

'Napoleon's Roads': *Heat*, Number 2 (new series), 2001, and *The Kenyon Review*, Volume XXV, Number 3/4, 2003.

'Kabul': *The Best Australian Stories 2002*, ed. Peter Craven, Black Inc., 2002, and *The Literature Quarterly*, Volume 45, Issue 1, 2001

'A': *Antipodes*, Volume 16, Issue 1, 2002.

'The Dead': Vagabond Press, 1999 and, translated by Nataša Kampmark, in *Priče iz Bezvremene Zemlje* (*Tales from a Timeless Country*), an anthology of Contemporary Australian prose (Agora: Zrenjanin, 2012).

'Crow Theses': *Southerly*, Volume 58, Issue 3, 1998.

'A Time of Strangers' (from 'Ten Short Pieces'): *Agenda Magazine*, Volume 41, Issues 1–2, 2005.

'The Wall': *Heat*, Number 5 (new series), 2003.

'The Lighthouse Keeper's Dream': *Best Stories Under the Sun*, ed. Michael Wilding, David A. Myers, Central Queensland University Press, 2004.

'A Traveller's Tale': *Hermes* (University of Sydney Union) 'Odyssey' issue, 2012.

'The Cellar': *The Warwick Review*, Volume 6, Issue 2, 2012.

'Swan': *The Best Australian Stories 2012*, ed. Sonya Hartnett, Black Inc., 2012.

'The Panther': *The Best Australian Stories 2014*, ed. Amanda Lohrey, Black Inc., 2014.

A number of these stories, translated by Nataša Miljković, have also appeared in *Atlas unutrašnjih suprotnosti* (*Atlas of the Inner Antipodes*), selected stories of David Brooks (Književna radionica Rašić: Belgrade, 2015).

AND TO THANK:

Madonna Duffy, wonderful publisher, and Jacqueline Blanchard, meticulous editor, and all other staff at UQP, and Tim Curnow, Teja Brooks Pribac, Aashish Kaul, Christopher Cyrill, Felicity Plunkett, Julie Clarke.

THE CONVERSATION

David Brooks

A novel brimming with mystery, confessions, food and philosophy

A young woman and an older man meet by accident – a gust of wind – at a restaurant in Trieste and find themselves dining together. They embark upon a conversation of the kind that can perhaps only happen between total strangers – risky, philosophical, full of the most intimate stories and confessions. She has questions. He finds, as the wine flows, delicious dishes come and go, and the velvet night deepens, that he doesn't have as many answers as he might have thought he had.

PRAISE FOR *THE CONVERSATION*

'Urbane and assured, *The Conversation* brilliantly examines modes of civility still possible in an adult world.' *Sydney Morning Herald*

'Rewarding for travellers, philosophers, wine-lovers and ravenous culture vultures' *Courier-Mail*

ISBN: 978 0 7022 4995 2

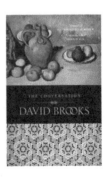